DAUGHTER OF VIOLENCE

This is a story of Anne of Warwick who was the last Plantagenet Queen of England. Her youth is woven with the double thread of happiness and anguish as she lives at the centre of a tumultuous civil struggle. Vibrant and content in Yorkshire, where she and Richard Plantagenet find the tender beginnings of love, she is abruptly forced into exile and a brutal marriage for political gain. Freed of this alliance by the savage battle of Tewkesbury, she is degraded and imprisoned by her own brother-in-law who covets her inheritance. Anne determines to win her way back to Yorkshire and Richard. She will defy her fate.

The tale swarms with people who are legends: Thomas Malory, author of *Le Morte d'Arthur*; Edward IV, the golden Plantagenet; Louis XI, the spider King of France; and Warwick the Kingmaker who uses his daughter as the fulcrum by which he resolves to change a world.

DAUGHTER OF VIOLENCE

PAULA SIMONDS

Patricia Pearson

ROBERT HALE · LONDON

© Paula Simonds 1981
First Published in Great Britain 1981

ISBN 0 7091 8990 7

Robert Hale Limited
Clerkenwell House
Clerkenwell Green
London EC1R 0HT

Photoset by
Specialised Offset Services Limited, Liverpool
Printed in Great Britain by
Clarke Doble & Brendon Ltd, Plymouth, Devon.
Bound by Redwood Burn Ltd

To my parents
Esther and Paul Simonds ...
With love

THE NEVILLES

Richard Neville, Earl of Warwick, the Kingmaker
Anne Beauchamp Neville, his wife – Countess of Warwick
Isabel Neville, his daughter – Duchess of Clarence
Anne Neville, his daughter – later Princess of Wales, Duchess of Gloucester
John Neville, his brother
George Neville, Archbishop of York, his brother

THE PLANTAGENETS

LANCASTER

Henry VI – disposed King of England, imprisoned in the Tower
Margaret of Anjou – his wife
Edward, Prince of Lancaster – son to Henry and Margaret

YORK

Edward IV – King of England
George, Duke of Clarence – brother to the King
Richard, Duke of Gloucester – brother to the King
Cicely, Duchess of York – mother to Edward IV, George and Richard

ANNE NEVILLE
1456-1485
QUEEN OF ENGLAND
Younger Daughter of Richard Earl
of Warwick called the Kingmaker
wife of the last Plantagenet King
RICHARD III
"In person she was seemly, amiable
and beauteous ... And according to the
interpretation of her name Anne full
gracious."
REQUIESCAT IN PACE

Anne's gravesite
Westminster Abbey

BOOK OF DAYS

PROLOGUE

"Fate will unwind as it must"
Beowulf

I

Childhood ended. Serenity shattered. Fear became the sum of Anne's being and her small body ached with it, this consuming terror which tore as icy as the winds of the April dawn. She had never known fear and it puzzled her that such an emotion could invade the great walls of Warwick and stab her whole world. She stood rigid; she was almost fifteen, a woman; her lips had not to quiver or her eyes to weep.

Isabel, her sister, wept. Their mother, Anne Beauchamp, prayed in the ancestral chapel. The Earl of Warwick, her father, gave orders. She watched him knowing ... she was a traitor's daughter. Her father in collusion with Isabel's husband, George of Clarence, had betrayed the King. And lost. Everything lost. Life and land forfeited they fled the King's angry justice.

Treason. No one said the word yet to Anne the bitter wind swirled it from gatehouse to curtain wall and about her father, all the while wailing the punishment was death. The small army of retainers abandoning the Clock Tower rooms, the emptying of the bridges and wall walks, the rattle of steel: It could not be happening. Not at Warwick. Not to her father.

Anne reached for him as he moved among the men, and he brushed her away. If only he would say, just once, it was all a misunderstanding, things would yet be well, and she would be free to live and love her Richard. She yearned to cry out, grab hold of his mailed arm, demand words of assurance. She did not. Silently, she stood in the doorway of Guy's Tower, out of the way, and waited.

A carriage swayed and lurched into the courtyard. Isabel could not ride horseback; she was eight months pregnant. Anne would travel with her sister, mother, and their servant, Ankarette Twynyho. A few fur wrappings were hastily thrown in the vehicle. The women scurried in. The countess still clutched a rosary, and Anne wondered her mother could grow so old in an hour's time. The girl looked once at her father. Fatigue and anguish streaked his face as mud streaked his armour.

If she had cried, it would have been for him. She loved him. He had achieved glorious victories, led mighty campaigns; but to her he was a warm, loving man who smelt of soft leather and held her in his lap. He had taught her to ride horseback. Once he had given her a lute and listened with obvious pleasure to her first, simple efforts. Sometimes he had told stories of the Danes and a time when their part of the world was wild, pagan Northumbria. They had listened for hours, as long as he could stay. It was such a little while ago and now her throat ached with uncried tears, and dread clutched coldly at her heart. The double portcullises crashed down behind them. Caesar's and Guy's Towers were misty in the dawn then lost in greyness. The great Clock Tower was visible for a few seconds longer before Warwick became a memory.

They rode for the port of Exeter. The carriage was a dark, jolting cave, unpadded, its hooped ceiling dark with age. They rested briefly at Cheltenham for Isabel suffered.

There, pacing about in anxiety and impatience, her father turned his anger on Anne.

"I had support you know, daughter."

The girl nodded warily.

"Lord Stanley, since he is my sister's husband, had vowed aid at Manchester."

"Lord Stanley, yes."

"Stanley's forces were routed by Richard."

"Richard of Gloucester!"

"An ingrate. He forgets the past. You. My kindnesses. He is the King's brother. Naught else."

A harsh, bitter anger contorted the Earl of Warwick's handsome face. The planes of his cheeks flattened; his mouth stretched to a thin line. He'd believed he had Richard, Duke of Gloucester, in his net. The duke had been raised at the family castle, Middleham, in Yorkshire, a small dark-haired boy who'd even then promised strength and purpose. And a happy boy, he would have staked his life on that. He'd trained him, cherished him, watched the first blossoming of love between the young duke and Anne. By all the saints, he'd liked the young man and been proud of him; for Richard was forged, even in those days, into a finer metal than most men. He was never expedient and once that had been a virtue. He could use such a man now, thought Warwick; and the earl's anger increased for he had forsaken steadfastness and trust in pursuit of fulfilment.

Anne swallowed. She saw rage. "I'm sorry, Father."

"If you'd married him …"

"I know." The paternal anger hurt. "Richard but waited upon the King's permission."

A fierce hate, bright as red coals, flamed in Warwick's eyes. "England has no King. Edward is unworthy."

She backed away. Shaken. She'd met Edward, her second cousin, once when Warwick had held him briefly as a prisoner at Middleham. He'd seemed a perfect King, tall, golden. Anne shook the image from her mind. A child's image. Yet Richard remained loyal to his eldest brother above all other loyalties. She glanced miserably at her father. He had betrayed his King, not her. "I'm sorry I couldn't help, Father."

For a moment, she knew it was there for one breath of time, he smiled gently. "You're a child, Anne. We'll see." He walked away. A busy man. Already full of new plans. His basic self-confidence stirred again.

Anne leaned against the coach. Fear. So much guilt. She heard her mother sobbing within the coach and Isabel's low moans mingling with Ankarette's murmurs. Would her marriage have changed this? The coldness that had seized her throat and body grew to pierce her brain, pounded behind her forehead. She climbed back into the coach. She had to serve her family. All else was confusion. Her father would care for them, perhaps in France; and she would be loyal in heart and mind.

Calais! A fresh, sea-scented breeze filled the painted sails and whipped to life the bear-and-ragged-staff banner. Anne shaded her eyes to see better the approaching harbour. Soon the sailors would pause briefly and sing a hymn of thanksgiving, offered to the Virgin of the Sea at the end of every voyage. Then the bells in the town would ring and cannons roar a salute. They'd be safe. She glanced at her father standing on the forecastle. His shoulders were thrown back, legs planted firmly, head high. She knew he thought of the glory days when he was Captain of Calais and a hero to all England. How young he looked, almost happy, as though boldness and optimism had been reborn.

It was a pity Isabel wasn't well enough to come on deck. She'd remember the Tower of Rysbank, which dominated the harbour, and the castles of Hammes and Guisnes standing sentinel at the entrance, just as they had seen them when very young. Calais was almost home. Here they could get off this ship, have good food, sleep in comfort. Perhaps Isabel would still be all right.

Anne was startled by the thunder. Salt water splashed onto the deck. The ship rocked. Such a small ship. They'd not been quick enough to get her father's flagship, *The Trinity*, although a number of smaller crafts with loyal men had joined them at Exeter. Thunder again and men scurried about. She knew the second time there was no welcome in Calais. The port was loyal to the King. They fired upon them.

Suddenly, breathlessly, her mother was at her side. "No!" She believed her own denial. Anne could see only puzzlement in her face, not fear. "No, it's but an overzealous welcome. John Wenlock, our friend, is in charge of the port." Anne Beauchamp, Countess of Warwick, had lived the past weeks in a nightmare she refused to accept. At Calais she could awaken. There, Wenlock, who had visited them often at Middleham and vowed his friendship, would give them refuge. Small and delicate, like her daughters, Anne Beauchamp had always been surrounded by vigorous, protective men so she'd approached her middle years with an unlined face and serenity. She'd never needed strength for more than the trivial, but she came of a proud bloodline and from somewhere found the stamina to say with calm reason: "It's a mistake. You'll see."

"They fired on us, Mama." The girl took her hand. "Let's go below. Isabel may need us."

Anne Beauchamp stared down at her travel-stained dress. "Wenlock is a friend."

"We've not been hit. Perhaps that is as much of a friend as he dares to be." Anne could hear the straining of the tiller and rudder as the ship began to change position. "Please, Mama, we should be below."

The countess half staggered. "Yes."

Below was a tiny, wainscoted cabin beneath the poop deck. The bunks were bone-crampingly narrow. Every creak of the tiller, every call to the helmsman, filled the tiny room with noise. Isabel lay on the best of the narrow bunks, her body bent, knees drawn up. Ankarette was with her, wiping perspiration from Isabel's forehead.

"Her time has come." Ankarette had been part of the family since Anne's infancy. The servant was pale as her sister. "Are there wine, herbs? The pains seize her. Often now. And hard."

Nausea and faintness rocked Anne. The sheets beneath Isabel's hips were red with blood. Her sister had always been delicate, a dainty blonde, never meant for childbearing on a ship's narrow bunk with cannon roaring.

Isabel's colourless lips screamed. "The pain. Please. Help me. I can't bear it."

Anne drew in her breath. And her sister had been proud, too. Proud as their father.

Isabel screamed again. "Christ. Holy Mother. Oh, mercy."

"Wine," Ankarette urged.

"I'll try." Anne climbed to the deck. The ship had pulled back. Their escort ships had slipped even further toward the safety of the open sea. Her father's face was flushed with fury. George of Clarence chewed on his lower lip. He looked sick. A galley, boldly decked in Yorkist pennants, pulled alongside the ship and a herald swung up the ladder. He was young, obviously uneasy, though he managed a minimal bow as he looked at some distant point over Warwick's shoulder, drew a rolled letter from beneath his tabard and read the incredible news. By royal proclamation, which had arrived half a day before, His Grace, King Edward, had ordered Calais closed to the Earl of Warwick. The Port of Calais was loyal to the King.

Her father stepped backward as though struck. His lips moved soundlessly. The small moment of stillness was broken by a thin cry of agony.

Anne pushed George forward. "Tell the herald to bring some wine from Calais. Wenlock will allow it. Tell him your wife suffers in childbirth."

George was limp, his voice a whine. "We need wine here. For my wife."

The herald, too young to remember the glory days of the Earl of Warwick, grew smug. A bunch of renegades who trailed lost reputations. He replied stiffly, "I am not authorized to bring any supplies."

"You're not in charge of Calais." Desperation pushed Anne even as she had pushed George. "Sir Wenlock won't treat us so. Ask him."

In the small area of the poop deck, Warwick moved close. His hand gripped the herald's shoulder, straining the cloth. "We must have wine. Hasten."

The herald attempted to shrug but faltered under the weight of that hand. He managed an ungracious bow. "As you say," he muttered. He was down the ladder and into the eight-oared galley in one quick motion. The galley pulled away with pennants blowing.

"May I see my wife, Anne?" George's eyes were red-rimmed, a muscle twitched in his left cheek. He held a shaking hand on the sleeve of her dress. "That scream. It was awful."

The girl took his arm. "Let's see. Perhaps for a moment. She's very weak."

At the door of the cabin Ankarette, arms crossed, filled the narrow entrance. She regarded George coldly. "This is woman's work, your grace."

George drew himself up as straight as the passage permitted. "Let me by, shrew. I'd see Isabel."

Ankarette shrugged. "Then you must be strong as a woman, lord." And you are a fool and weak, she thought in disgust. Her watchful hazel eyes regarded him with contempt.

Roughly George pushed her out of the way and, bending, entered the tiny cabin. Anne stood by the door. Isabel lay on her side amidst fouled sheets which the countess was attempting to change. Through dry, cracked lips her breathing came, panting and animal-like. A blue vein pulsed sluggishly across her forehead, the only colour in the puffy whiteness of her face. George took a deep breath, as did Anne, and they both choked on the stench of vomit and birth-blood. George put one hand forward to touch Isabel, then clutched his own stomach and fled.

For a brief moment Anne felt a flicker of amusement and pity. She turned to her mother and Ankarette. "Wine has been ordered. I'm sure Wenlock will send some."

Her mother nodded. "Of course he will. John Wenlock is a friend." She looked about the small cabin and at Isabel. "I do not understand this day."

Ankarette unbound her hair under her coif. She was careful to tie no knots. Then she opened the door of the cabin slightly. "Nothing must be sealed," she whispered.

Slowly Anne undid the plaits of her own hair. Ankarette was right. Anything that could help had to be done. No breeze stirred on the scorched air. Anne's hair clung damply to her neck and arms. She knew death was near.

She smelled it in the blood, the heavy air, the ships old timbers. She remembered Isabel radiant in a gown of white velvet during the Yuletide season. It seemed an unreal dream.

She helped apply cool compresses to Isabel's forehead and body, massage the muscles of her back and moisten her lips with water. By the time wine arrived Isabel no longer cried out and her face had grown a death-like grey with the sharp lines of the bones clear against the skin. Ankarette forced some wine between Isabel's teeth.

"All will be well, little lady," the servant murmured. "I will take care." Her figure, strong and protective, bent over Isabel.

Isabel coughed on the wine. "The babe." Her voice was a tiny whisper. "It's dead. Not moved. Three days. I know." She gasped, swallowed, then arched her back in a spasm of pain.

Ankarette leaned closer. "Forgive me, my dearest lady. I must hurt you so."

II

Isabel lived, drifting in and out of a world of pain and fantasy. Once she murmured: "I dreamed it moved. My baby. I loved it."

Her mother and Ankarette tended her. "There will be others," they consoled. " 'Tis not your fault." The countess took her rosary out, but let it lie, a pool of coral beads in her lap.

Anne prepared it for burial, the tiny, wizened body, so perfect and still. There was a bit of blond fuzz upon the head and she was sure the eyes, which would never open, were blue. She was not repulsed by this tiny, dead thing, but performed the ritual in numbness. Gently she wrapped the babe in a piece of Isabel's petticoat, covering it completely except for one miniature hand lying upon the folds. She looked questioningly at her sister, wondering if Isabel would like to see the child; but the young woman had drifted into a restless sleep and Ankarette shook her head.

"It's better a mother not see a still-born one," she whispered.

So Anne took the tiny bundle and climbed to the deck. It was evening now and a breeze pulled at her skirts and unbound hair while the sun hung low and red on the rim of the ocean, turning the water to rippling flame. She stood there with the dead child and tried to accept that this child would never see the sun or know one brief smiling moment. He had been loved, loved by Isabel while he lived within her. Loved by all as the first of a new generation. And he had given joy to Isabel until the end. Now, though unbaptized, he was surely with the angels, yet no one had ever kissed him or sung a single lullaby. Gently, Anne kissed the small, cold hand. "Little, unnamed boy," she prayed, "may the angels sing you your lullaby."

Late that night while Isabel slept, two sailors lowered the tiny body over the side. Anne stood by George who sobbed; his breath wine-drenched, the child was to have been his prince and heir. Warwick, head bowed, watched the small form sink into the waves. His grandson. The countess wept and made the sign of the cross pledging special prayers every April 16. Below in the cabin, watched over by Ankarette, Isabel did not know. And Anne, her lips as cold as the baby's hand, allowed the sadness she had held at bay to escape and fill her. Her thoughts followed the child into the water, plunging with it into the depths of that endlessly rocking cradle.

Anne was on deck when they landed at Honfleur, a French port, still the governor of the region was the Count of St Pol, the uncle of King Edward's spiteful queen, Elizabeth Woodville. Strangely, there was no challenge. Seagulls circled and squawked above them. A snatch of music drifted across the harbour from a tavern near the docks, followed by singing and the resounding thump of the tabor. It would be much the same in England in the spring. England – home.

"Well, daughter, you find the scene pleasing?" Anne was startled. Both her father and brother-in-law had joined her at the rail. They were finely dressed. The chain about

Warwick's shoulders was worth a fortune, a Burgundian fortune. George sported a handsome gold medal of St George in his cap. They'd raided as pirates the past months.

"Yes. I'm glad to land." She didn't show her puzzlement. Warwick looked exhilarated, a man about to start a great new venture.

"Louis of France won't be glad to see our ships here in St Pol's domain." George obviously didn't share this euphoria.

"Louis won't care. He hates Burgundy, especially its Duke Charles, whom we robbed. He'll welcome us." Warwick smiled a little. "I have his word on it."

"And the treaty of Peronne with Charles of Burgundy?" George chewed on his lip.

Her father widened his arms expansively. "King Louis doesn't rule France by being tied to unfavourable treaties. He'll like my plan, no, call it an enterprise, the Enterprise of England."

The girl turned away. She knew nothing of treaties and only a little of Louis. The French King was a much feared and respected man. She climbed down to their cabin then paused for George had followed her. In the dim light his face was creased with disappointment.

Once again pity flickered. "George, are you all right? We're soon to land."

"It is nothing to me. I'm no longer in the plan of things. I'm no longer promised a crown." He pressed his hands against his head as though to block out the thought. "Damnation! For what did I give up everything?"

"George, nothing is resolved. It is a long way from here to London. Whatever my father plans you'll be included as Isabel's husband."

"What about as King Edward's brother?" His face

twisted. "God, why was I not born first?" His mood shifted again. "I'd see my wife."

"Isabel sleeps. Surely you can wait a few hours."

Ankarette appeared. Her candle cast its uneven light as she raised it. "The countess sleeps, too." She shifted her cool gaze to George. "The Lady Isabel is not ready to resume her duties as a wife. It's a wonder she had no childbed fever. A miracle, in truth."

George struck Ankarette across the face, his heavy ring gashing a jagged cut. "Slut, all this woman talk. I will see my wife. You can't stop me."

Anne could have hit him then. She grabbed the candle from Ankarette and thrust it close to his face. "You'll not take out your disappointments on Isabel or any of us, George. Act like your patron saint. He fought dragons."

"You all conspire against me. You, this servant-witch, my own brothers." He shielded his eyes from the candle. "I am next in line to the throne. Edward's brother, heir. Doesn't that count for anything?"

"Not if you are under attainder," Anne said slowly.

George looked wildly about. His handsome, weak face gleamed in the sinister half-light. "I hate you all. You'll regret my hate."

Anne turned to Ankarette and forced calmness. "Let us wash your cheek. Face wounds always bleed so."

Ankarette nodded. "He's drunk. It doesn't matter."

"Everything I do matters." George almost sobbed. "No one thinks I count. They will find out their error in Hell." George turned from them, his shoulders shaking. "I will never be King."

Anne looked at him and Ankarette's face and hoped he was right.

Indeed George, Duke of Clarence, had guessed the truth

closely enough. The Enterprise of England had no place for him. Warwick explained his great new venture to his youngest daughter as they rested in a white-plastered nunnery in Honfleur. The Virgin Mary smiled sweetly down, there were summer flowers on the tables, roses, white roses for York, Anne thought to herself.

"So I am joining forces with the Lancastrians who have been exiled here in France." Warwick paced about the small parlour as he spoke. "Margaret of Anjou protests, of course."

"You fought her and her Lancastrians and won, Father." The girl waited uneasily. All her childhood she had heard of bitter, but victorious, battles against the Lancastrians and the merciless leadership of Margaret of Anjou. This woman had led troops into battles herself and ordered Richard's father and seventeen-year-old brother killed with a wave of her hand.

Warwick put his arm about Anne's waist, drawing her close. "Listen, daughter, Margaret writes: 'The Earl of Warwick has pierced my heart with wounds which can never be healed; they will bleed till the day of judgment when I will appeal to the justice of God for vengeance against him'."

"You told me she always spoke in fits of passion." Anne leaned against her father, trying to feel warm closeness instead of unease. "Yet I don't wonder. Her husband rots in the Tower because of you. After all, he was anointed Henry the Sixth. Her son has grown up in France without inheritance." She looked up at her father, trying to read his face. "You often said she brought it all down upon herself, that the English would have tolerated Henry forever but for the injustices of his Queen. I remember you said rebellion was a patriotic duty." Warwick had grown restless as she spoke; anger flushed his face. Anne finished in dull dismay.

"You won the crown for Edward. The rightful King."

Her father brushed away all statements. But he considered her youth and was patient. "Child, everything has changed. I would put Henry VI back on the throne and govern through him. Thus good government. And we'll have our estates and all that is ours."

"Edward IV and the Yorkists won't just vanish."

"I need but one victory. Edward killed. He is only a man, after all. Richard killed so there is no line of succession. George can be managed. Perhaps he'll be content with his dukedom."

A sickness grew within her threatening to rise and check her voice. "You would do this, Father? Henry VI is lack-witted, has been for years. You told me. Margaret killed your own kin. She hates you. The Lancastrians must hate you. Edward, Richard – you were their mentor, their friend."

Warwick shrugged. Anne didn't think he heard her. "Old emotions. Old memories. They've no place here. Should I be held back when I can go forward? Recover all, and more?"

"More." She leaned against the window-sill. The room was full of shadows. "What else is there?"

He took her hand; his voice became soft, tender. "Anne, sweetheart, listen. I'll put the royal woolsack, Henry VI, back on the throne. He will be my tool. Margaret, too, must follow where I lead; for I command the military. I will have such power." He paused, standing so close she could smell the soft leather of his clothes, his fine new boots. "And you'll have power. You, Anne."

"Power?" The word tasted strangely in her mouth.

"Yes, for you will marry Margaret and Henry's son. He is almost eighteen. Handsome, so I'm told. A trained warrior. And someday he will be King. And you, daughter, the Queen and mother to a line of kings."

"No. I do not want that. God, no."

Warwick didn't hear her. So blindingly bright had his future become he was impervious, eager only for the next turn of fortune's glittering wheel.

"It's all arranged. Louis of France, he is Margaret's first cousin, pleads my cause in this." He laughed. "Rather destined, I believe. For you, Anne, the greatest prize of all. Your dowry is England." He lifted her up, swirled her about as a child is swirled.

She screamed then. "No! Can't you hear? I want none of it?"

His laughter faded. "You will do as you are told."

"I will not marry this Prince of Lancaster. I will join in no plot to kill Richard."

Warwick took a deep breath, became gentle. "Anne, you have my stubborn streak. The line of your chin, just so I looked as a boy. Well, pride is well and good; but this is not a simple world of right and wrong. Everything is shaded, twisted, turned about. My honour now lies with Lancaster. Would you gainsay me the chance to be premier lord of England once more?"

She shook her head silently.

"Then marry a handsome young man. Is that so hard?"

"Father, please don't ask it." The girl took his hand and pressed it against her cheek. "Anything but that." She sank to her knees. He had to hear her.

Her father jerked his hand away. "I don't ask. I order."

Anne stood. Anger hardened her voice. "Margaret of Anjou hates us. No doubt her son does, too. She will never consent to such a marriage."

"She'll consent. I told you King Louis would see to it."

Her anguish broke through. "Father, how can you? You served York, loved and served. Lancastrian rule was evil.

You told me yourself." She wanted to stop and could not. "How can you betray yourself this way?"

He did not touch her. There was no expression on his face, none at all. "Anne, this is my choice. You, remember it well, have no choice."

BOOK OF DAYS

Part I – 1470-71

The Daemon Lover

"O what hills are yon, you pleasant hills,
    That the suns shines sweetly on?"
"O yon are the hills of heaven," he said,
"Where you will never win."

"O whaten a mountain is yon," she said,
    "All so dreary wi frost and snow?"
"O yon is the mountain of hell," he cried,
    "Where you and I will go.

                   Medieval Ballad
                   "The Daemon Lover"

I

Cursing the baleful summer thunder, the townspeople of Angers tried to sleep. From the brooding ancient castle the royal Fleur-de-lis flapped in the wind like a trapped bird. The King of France was in residence.

Anne Neville lay sleepless on a prickly mattress. To her the castle was a tomb. Its air stank with mold and duplicity and hate. Its courtyard, she remembered, reeked with dog-dung. Time had stopped in the darkness, trapping her in this evil place. She stared at the window slits, seeing beyond Angers to freedom, another country, *her* country. England. Home.

Never would this strange land, which sheltered the banished Lancastrians, be anything but an exile. Anne shivered in a tightening grip of dread. She wanted to bolt the bed, flee into the shadows away from the scheming forces gathered together in this castle. She couldn't move. She, Anne Neville of Warwick, was trapped. Fear had slammed the door to action. Helpless, ensnared as a tiny insect in the web woven by her own father as well as King Louis XI, exiled Margaret of Anjou and Edward, her son. They each played their own great games. Except her. She was the pawn.

Bought and sold by her own father into a lifetime of

enduring Margaret's loathing. The woman who wore black, led armies, killed. She'd snarled whispered words of hate at dinner that very evening, even as the minstrels played and Anne stirred slabs of meat drifting in heavy sauces. Margaret would never forget or forgive her for being young, Warwick's daughter, the bride chosen for her son. The mockery of the son meant nothing. "Virgin meat is tasty," he'd said and grinned at them all.

Anne drew on memory for strength. She'd been loved. At Middleham. On a summer day Richard had woven her a crown of clover, jewelled with yellow celandine. They'd frolicked as puppies among the purple thistles of cool Yorkshire. Later at Warwick castle Richard had spoken shyly of his love for her. Vowed marriage someday. Neither had planned further. They were children, innocents, the older Anne realized. They knew nothing.

Abruptly, Anne's thoughts were jerked back to the bedchamber. The massive door opened, allowing a moment of light from the torch-lit corridor, then thudded shut. Anne's heart constricted, her breath was a small gasp. Fleetingly she hoped the intruder was her mother, but the woman who bent over her had red-rimmed eyes, the only colour in a face of grey.

"God's mercy!" Anne pulled the bedclothes and her long hair about her nakedness.

"So, Warwick's daughter. Didn't you know I'd come? Snivelling, puny slut."

Horror alerted all Anne's muscles. She sat up holding the sheets about her. "Madame, why taunt me? I want no part in this. England knows peace."

Margaret laughed silently. Warwick's daughter. The man she'd fought. The Kingmaker. Damn him. He'd taken her husband's crown for another. He and his Yorkist friends. Now was *her* time.

The light from Margaret's candle darted about. "I'll rack your England, turn it to an island of blood. Until my husband is on the throne. My son acknowledged heir." The Queen's breathing quickened. "All humbled. Every Yorkist rotting in their grave."

She bent over Anne and the girl could smell the sweaty flesh, the stink of decaying teeth. "Do you know, Warwick's daughter, your father apologized to me, on his knees, *his knees*, for his past allegiance to York." Scornful, putrid words burned against Anne's face. "He thinks to gain back power in my cause. A Lancastrian. The Devil has his jest." The candle flickered wildly.

Margaret thought with rage of Anne's youth. The first delicate shimmering of her beauty was cause added to bitter justification to kill. She'd never paused to consider consequences before. Why hesitate now?

Anne would not let this woman see her cry, not this night, not ever. She lifted her face, her chin firm. "Madame, leave me. You're not worth hating."

Margaret spat. Red spotted her cheeks. "Jade. Damn you to Hell." The girl must die ... Now ... While vulnerable. One Yorkist dead.

Anne wiped the hot spittle from her cheek. She guessed Margaret's thoughts. The Queen who killed. God help her. She searched in the darkness for her night robe. "Let me alone. I'll go away."

The candle crept close. "Away. To Hell. Burn in Hell, little bitch who'd be queen."

Anne put her hands in front of her face to block the curse, the piercing malevolence. Her numbed mind lost the battle to terror. Death was coming. The woman was mad. She couldn't scream. She waited. Condemned, yet seeking a chance. Any escape.

Margaret yanked aside the sheets. "Skinny slut. My son

wants you. I must tell him." The grating voice turned to mockery. "You had small, pointy teats, pubis of a child. Cry, damn you."

"Have done!" Anne pushed the candle aside. In an instant the tiny, jumping flame caught the crisp taffeta bed-hangings. Another second and a quick burning fire raced up the fabric.

Margaret stepped back. Her eyes were bright. "God hears me. Your hair, it burns. You'll burn." In her mind the woman could see the girl encircled in flames. The small white body would turn dark, the flesh would melt. How she'd scream before she died!

Agile with desperation, Anne jumped from the bed and grabbed her dressing-gown from a wall peg. She pulled the robe over her head, forcing the smoldering ends of hair against her skin under the gown. She'd no time for pain. The mattress was already patchy with small fires. The heat and flames began a deadly murmur. Smoke thickened blackly so the girl stumbled as she felt frantically for the door. Acrid air stung in her nose and throat, her eyes were dimmed by sooty fumes. The door was heavy. "Help," she called. "For the love of God. Help!"

Margaret watched the fire. The murmur became a low roar. Fragments of bed-curtains drifted down, a gentle snow in a world of scorching heat. The floor rushes had begun to catch and dense, stifling smoke curled upward.

Anne pulled at the door. "Do you want to die? To burn? Christ! Help me!"

Slowly Margaret turned. One hand gripped Anne's arm in a band of steel. "You will die, Anne of Warwick. 'Tis God's will."

Anne screamed. Pain tore at her shoulder and down the length of her arm as she tried to twist free. She coughed. "Murderer."

"For my son ... I'd kill a world." Margaret, too, choked on smoke. She pulled the door ajar, pushed Anne from her, back into the burning room.

Anne staggered. The fire burned in her chest. Smoke smothered her voice. With the desperate quickness of youth she ran past Margaret, through the slit of the door. The inrushing air from the hall was cool. Anne stumbled, clung to the wall, trying to see beyond the fog stinging her eyes. "*Au secours*," she whispered to the dark tunnel of corridor. "Fire. *Feu*. Help."

She could see the floor rushes, catching the fresh air, turning to tiny seas of flame.

Margaret walked by her. The woman's face was streaked with ashes, drawn with fury. She stared at Anne. "Hell will find you another time." She hoped the girl might yet die. Smoke could kill. A little smile twisted her face. "Or I'll find you."

Anne slammed the door shut. The whole castle could burn if someone didn't come soon. "*Au secours*," she cried again and choked on the dust in her throat.

It was Olivier, a humpbacked servant, who answered. From what seemed a far distance she heard him say, "Damoiselle, you're burned. I've an oinment. I'm the King's barber-surgeon."

Anne sank down against the wall. "The fire." She trembled and couldn't stop.

Olivier nodded. Anne was dimly aware that from somewhere buckets of sand arrived. Men went into the room with thick blankets, holding damp cloths over their faces. She sat with her head between her knees, fighting faintness. Margaret was gone. She'd slipped into the shadows.

"I thought I heard you cry. I smelled smoke." Olivier's voice was amazingly gentle. "I'll get some ladies to attend you. And the ointment. I make it myself."

"*Merci*." She blinked, trying to clearly see him, this gargoyle of salvation. "Thank God you came."

"Damoiselle, you are brave."

"No, I'm afraid. All the time. I got out only because Margaret didn't want to die and I was too quick for her."

"Damoiselle, you're small ... delicate. She's all sinewy muscle. She could have forced you back."

Anne closed her stinging eyes. "I wouldn't let her."

"So she must have known." Olivier looked down at the girl. A pathetic child. Warwick should have had sons. The barber-surgeon shrugged. She didn't cry, this girl-child. He had to tell the King. A brave one. She could come to matter.

In far off London the summer thunder rumbled, too. Richard could hear the heavy drops of rain spattering into the swollen Thames. He waited. Edward IV, the royal Plantagenet, appeared to his youngest brother as a tawny lion. Lazy as the real lions guarding the Tower gate. Wrapped in silks, comfortably ensconced in a mound of pillows, long legs stretched out, he ate date after date, spitting the pits aside. Beyond the door the noises of Westminster beckoned: laughter, singing, somewhere a lute, the patter of dancing from the Great Hall. Queen Elizabeth Woodville had a new jester.

"And there's no news of Warwick?" Richard could wait no longer. Any minute might bring interruptions. Then Edward would assume his jovial or cynical or amorous mask and be unreachable.

"Not this week. No doubt he and Louis hatch schemes. My spies keep me informed." The King smiled at his brother. Richard was eighteen. The only man in the kingdom he totally trusted. And loved. His short, dark-haired brother. Richard looked like their father. God rest his soul.

"And the Lady Anne?"

"Forget her, Dick. Take up tennis. Better yet, a mistress. I've one so rounded, plump as a plover. She's yours."

"I'd hoped to marry Anne Neville." Richard knew the court laughed at him for his dreary musings on Warwick and right and wrong. Only Edward knew of his love for Anne. He, too, wished he could forget. He had tried to block out the years at Middleham, Warwick's patient tutelage in the tiltyard. All the skills of warfare he possessed came from the man now an enemy.

Edward spit out another date-pit. "Richard, listen. Do you think Warwick would turn from his course now, even if I asked him? He's a shooting star. I'm sorry. He was my friend, too."

"Then we must prepare for battle."

"I suppose so." Edward yawned. "The country is weary of battles. I wonder if they'll rally for Warwick when allied with Margaret of Anjou? A savage kinship. It should be sealed by pens dipped in blood." Edward remembered how Margaret had executed his father and impaled the mutilated head on Micklegate Bar, one of the gates of York. She'd killed a brother, too, a boy of seventeen. She'd almost killed England.

"Sealed in blood." Richard had turned pale. "Edward, don't you see, Warwick is going to marry little Anne to Margaret's son. It's her blood."

Anguish twisted in him. Anne. Defenceless. Barely fifteen. He would have cared for her, cherished her.

"Margaret will resist such a union, Richard."

"And Louis will persuade her. I've heard he could charm Gabriel to petition God."

"I saw Anne a few years ago." Edward spoke quietly. "When her father held me prisoner. She was such a tiny thing. Delicate. A lovely bird. She was shy of me, even with guards thick as fleas. I must have a dubious reputation with the ladies."

"You do. And you like it." Richard smiled. He was used to hiding emotions. He loathed his brother's court. He believed the vicious frivolity of Westminster was a malignancy at the centre of the realm. Woodville greed was insatiable. Cruelty amused the Queen and her kin. Lies flowed as wine. Yet Woodvilles always flattered, charmed Edward.

"Dick, I wish there was a way to help you. I see none." Edward watched carefully. He wondered what Richard thought. Would his youngest brother accept this inaction? The King knew he accepted a great deal simply out of love. Richard was a Libra. Venus ruled him. Such a birthdate explained his uniqueness. Richard was deeper than the Thames. Few realized it, though. They thought him simply blind.

"I'll send my tart to your bed. She'll purge you of this calf-love." Edward didn't think the ploy would work, but he could imagine no other. Not with the candles burning low and sweetly scented. The pillows fluffed. And he had several mistresses.

"No tart, Edward. I can find my own. You'll offer Warwick life if he comes against you?"

"I'll offer him life. God. I'm not made of stone. When I have sons, Richard, let no man become their kingmaker."

"And Anne?"

"Brother, she may be a wife. I say again, forget her."

II

In the morning Anne finally spoke with her father alone. They rode to the cathedral of Angers, noticing only the clear sunlight, ignoring the curious stares of the people setting up their shops and arranging wares, the redolence of onions, the mounds of yesterday's decay and filth being haphazardly pushed into piles. Warwick expected the French to gawk. They were used to their shabby King, who dressed like a tradesman and pinned lead medals in his cap. He, the Earl of Warwick, wore a satin doublet accenting his wide shoulders. Above dyed leather boots, hose clung to the hard muscles of his legs. He fingered a thick, gold chain, in the traditional SSS design of Lancaster. "A gift from Louis," he explained to his daughter. His forty-one-year-old face was young, exuberant. "A token of esteem and support."

Anne couldn't look at him. In her mind English voices cried "A Warwick" and his banner of the Bear and Ragged Staff lifted on the wind. A hero's banner for the premier noble of the land. Such a little while ago.

Warwick ignored her silence. "The great days will come again. And there'll be no fickle Edward to gainsay me. He betrayed me by his secret marriage to the Woodville, his lack of trust. God is just. I made Edward a King. I'll crown Lancaster again. Forget old enmities, Anne. Scorpio with its red star, my star, is high. The scorpion will sting York till they run away." He smiled at Anne. He'd hoped she would laugh.

Anne didn't seem to hear him. Ahead loomed the spired cathedral. At its entrance the earl helped his daughter dismount and led her gently down the long centre nave to the high altar. Stained-glass windows splashed multi-coloured patterns across the sanctuary. A priest, soundlessly moving on bare feet, approached with a gold cross in the crystal centre of which Anne could see a splinter of dark wood.

"As you requested, my lord," the tonsured head turned blue in the light, "our most holy treasure, the Cross of St Laud d'Angers. See the blessed piece of our Saviour's own sacred cross."

Anne gazed in wonderment. The dark splinter must have been stained with the very blood of the crucified Christ. She concentrated on the precious relic until it blurred. "Does it work miracles?"

"No, daughter." Warwick answered for the priest had moved away, leaving the cross on the altar. "Yet it has great power. Anyone swearing on this cross and then perjuring himself will die within the year."

Anne nodded. "A fearful relic."

"Listen, daughter. On this cross on the twenty-fifth of July, I swore to uphold the party and righteous quarrel of King Henry of Lancaster. And more – I pledged your betrothal to Edward, Prince of Wales, son of Margaret and Henry, as a sealing of the bargain for the Enterprise of England. Do you understand?" His hands were heavy on her shoulders. "On this cross."

"I understand. You'll die if you forswear your vow." The

cathedral darkened as a cloud hid the sun. In a side chapel someone chanted, "*Miserere mei Deus.*"

"And you too will vow. So doubly bind the oath. A covenant you dare not break." Warwick knew his daughter, knew she might rebel.

Anne faced her imperious father. "Don't you know? Care? Margaret cursed me. Tried to kill me. The fire. You must know. She was sure I'd die. She wanted me to. I'll not marry into a life of hate." She tried to pray the chanted words. "Have mercy upon me, O God."

"The fire was surely an accident." Warwick became mild, cajoling. "Margaret is obsessed with Hell and damnation. When she saw the flames her brain fevered. You don't understand these things. Pledge your troth, daughter."

Anne winced, diminished by the intensity of his command. Everything towered above her; her father, the choir-stalls, the arched ceiling. She struggled against fatigue and pain. A scattering of burns, two deeply red and moist, smarted on her back. Her shoulder was swollen and bruised. It had taken several hours of ministrations by chambermaids to clean the soot from her body. Even now the smoky aroma lingered. Not for some political scheme called the Enterprise of England would she face such a night again. "You don't need me." She took a deep breath and dared the ultimate reason. "I would marry Richard. I love him."

"Silly chit." Warwick held his anger at bay. "Richard is part of the court. No doubt he keeps a mistress. Why would he think of you any more?"

"He wanted to marry me. The last time at Warwick."

The pressure of his hands increased. "Forget him. He's brother to a King who discredits my greatness. He'll be killed or executed. Let others arrange lives."

"It's my life."

"Ridiculous. A child must honour its parents. Marry as ordered. So it is commanded by God."

Anne glanced at the cross. "I think God has little to do with your Enterprise."

Her father shook her roughly. "I told you. You have only one sentence to say." His voice was hoarse. "Pledge yourself as bride of Edward of Lancaster. Here. On this cross."

"No. Never." She gazed up at him, the banished tears filling her eyes. "Please, let me go to a nunnery."

"By God, Anne. Wouldn't you see Warwick again, and Middleham? Think of your mother. Should she live in exile? And your sister? I will win back all. I've told you. The Lancastrians are simply tools. I'll command the military. So the realm. My rule. Strong. Just. Such power!"

The sleepless night, the time of terror, were heavy as his grip. "I can't. Father, I beg you, make your peace with England, with King Edward. Let's go back to the days when life was happy, right." Her words sank to a whisper. "Father, your honour ..."

Warwick raised his hand. His rings flashed. Suddenly he stopped and the blow never came. He knew, with a certain pride, she was too much like him. A beating would change nothing. He took a deep breath.

"Anne, you've no choice." He became calm, a concerned father. "I see in your face something of myself as a boy. Your eyes, like mine, filled with resolve and strength. So, Anne, do this in pride. A duty well done. A recompense for the years at Middleham. Remember the days I taught you to ride horseback? How you played the lute most evenings. Think of those good days, years."

He folded her in his arms. "Little one, sweetheart. It's truly for the best. Would I harm you? The Anjou woman won't live forever. The Prince is only seventeen. You, my daughter, will be Queen and reign in such glory." He kissed her forehead. "For your mother, for me. For all we have shared."

He waited. She was a child in his arms. Only a few years ago she had been a baby, bright with dimpled smiles between two fair braids. For a moment he saw himself, younger, totally at ease in a world where trust and friendship were the pattern. That world no longer existed, not for him. He had become a legend; he had to live it out. For a brief moment he perceived somehow he was trapped in his own dream of himself.

Anne cried. Then, helpless, vulnerable to gentleness, she reached forward and touched the crystal centre of the cross. "I pledge myself to Edward of Lancaster."

Patiently, her father held her until she could stop the heavy, racking sobs. She wept for them all, for a time forever lost, a love never to be known. She did not try and explain.

On the stony road to Amboise, Prince Edward swore violently. He didn't whip the horse. Mars was the one perfect thing he possessed, white as snow, a stallion for a king. In fact the horse was a loan from Louis, but Edward didn't think of such unpleasantries.

"Why leave?" he demanded for the third time. "I like the Neville mouse."

"She's no mouse." Margaret glared up at her son from her own mare. "I told you. I accidentally knocked over a candle in her solar. She will spread the rumour I tried to kill her, burn down the castle. All sorts of wild nonsense."

"Lies?" Edward eyed his mother shrewdly.

"I'd kill Warwick. A blade through the heart and done with pleasure. The girl is nothing."

"Warwick is your guide back to the throne. The girl's my bride. Will she come to Amboise in the week?"

"Probably." Margaret wondered how much more she could endure. The last nine years she had lived, her heart had beat, for her son. His tutor had tried to mention weaknesses, he had dared say faults. Margaret hadn't listened. Edward was perfect. How could he want the Neville chit? She hated the girl for that alone. Let him take village women to toss in the sweaty embrace men needed. She thought of Edward with his loins pressed against Anne Neville's white skin.

"When will we go to fight? I want to kill. God, life is dull."

Margaret glanced up at her son through her eyelashes, a trick she had mastered long ago when men had declared themselves slain by Cupid's arrows from such a glance. Men were fools. "The little Neville's a narrow-hipped bitch, Edward."

The Prince thumped his horse. "A tight squeeze. All the better."

Margaret was seldom aware of her son's mockery. This she heard and a cold fury coalesced about her heart. The girl should pay. She would serve a purpose first, though.

"Then I may wed, bed and be off to England." Edward's colour was high with excitement.

"It may be some weeks. The nuptial dispensation, you know. A pity." Margaret smiled serenely. "Only the advance goes to England. You'll follow when all is secure."

"I should be in the forefront. With Warwick and Oxford."

My son, I'm going to keep you safe if I have to chain you, Margaret thought. She said pleasantly, "Your place is by my side."

"My place is in England where I'll be Prince of Wales."

"But think how lonesome the little Neville would be."
Margaret shaped the words calmly. Rage and ravished
pride hid behind her lowered eyes. Her son might stay
willingly for Warwick's chit of a daughter. "Neville blood
runs hot, no doubt," she added with scorn.

Edward grinned. "It would be a sin to leave a virgin."

"You must think of ways to take her virginity.
Memorable ways. Some women like one caress, some
another. Many find pain joyous." Margaret glanced
sideways again. Her son's face was flushed. She could see
his erection through the lines of his codpiece. So Anne
Neville would cry, she hoped. Night after night. And when
England was truly won the girl would die.

III

Anne didn't talk with her father again. The first week of August he rode off accompanied by Lancastrian exiles, French mercenaries and a heavy bag of French gold. His countess gave him the stirrup-cup in the courtyard at Angers. Anne waved. She knew he didn't see her. Already his vision was fastened on the future, on England.

Her mother came to her as the cavalcade cleared the draw-bridge. The countess smiled bravely. "A bold sight, daughter." In her heart the countess wanted to lie on the filthy paving-stones and weep. A desperate gamble. A route without middle ground. All won – or lost.

"Yes, Mama. He looked splendid." Anne felt a touch of the old admiration. By St George, her father would dare the world.

"I'll miss him so." The countess crossed herself. "God willing, we'll spend Christmas in Warwick and I'll light candles in the chapel of my ancestors."

"Did father tell you of Margaret, the fire?" Anne immediately regretted the question. Happy anticipation faded from her mother's face. "No. He told me you were in accord with the Enterprise of England. No more. Margaret and her son left Angers the day after we dined together. They've gone on to Amboise."

"You know of the marriage I vowed?"

"By which, through the might of your father's sword, you'll become Princess of Wales. Love comes after marriage, Anne. Child, I know it's hard for you."

She stopped as John de Vere, thirteenth Earl of Oxford and Anne's uncle by marriage, bowed before them with a flourish. "I'm to return to Amboise today. I've heard the Prince most eagerly awaits you, Damoiselle. As would any man. I envy Edward of Lancaster." His words slithered about smooth as silk. "Then I leave for a triumph in England. Finally, Lancaster comes again."

The countess nodded. It was hard to think of de Vere as an ally. He had for so long been one of the resourceful and dreaded enemies. "We will go to Amboise in a few days." She managed politeness, after all he now fought in her husband's cause. "I would have Anne meet our hostess, Queen Charlotte."

De Vere bowed, his cap sweeping the ground. "I'll tell the Prince you are eager as he. Youth. Such a happy time." Oxford cared nought if Anne were happy or mourned. He merely played his expected role and they all knew it.

Charlotte of Savoy was not one of the role-players. She was changing napkins on her spindly son when Anne and her mother entered. She held up the baby whose overlarge head lolled and whose legs to others seemed ominously curved. After two daughters God had given her a son. She saw the baby as perfect.

"They tell me he looks just like his father at a month's age." Charlotte sat down and nuzzled the infant. "So this is the little bride. Tell me about yourself, *ma petite*."

Anne had heard Charlotte was kind; she'd planned each word carefully. "Madame, first let me congratulate you on your handsome son."

"Indeed yes. France is blessed in having a Dauphin."

The countess watched Anne uneasily. She'd never seen her daughter appear so determined. Every muscle in her young face was tense.

"As for myself, Madame, I ask your counsel." Anne took a deep breath. "My vow on the cross of St Laud should be absolved. I was confused. I acted without thought. Surely such a pledge is not binding."

"Anne!" The countess gasped. "Your father ... his plans."

"He doesn't need me. I'll go to a nunnery. Isabel rests at Honfleur. I could join her." Anne held herself in tight control. She didn't dare add her secret hope of finding passage to England, though the idea beckoned intensely as a constant, but distant, summer song.

"My dear child." Charlotte patted Anne's arm. "No one could absolve you from such a vow. On the true cross!" The Queen thought back to her own youthful marriage. This girl was lovely as a spring flower though and she had been a plump and placid creature. "The years go by so quickly," she said slowly. "You'll forget your misgivings and find joy in your children."

"Madame, I beg you. You are Queen. The Pope ..."

"Would not let you forswear your vow, hazard your soul." Charlotte knew she must tell Louis to have a watch kept on this girl. She sensed a daring desperation. A few men-at-arms should accompany them to Amboise.

"Anne will do as her father wishes." The countess put her arm around her daughter's shoulders. "He knows what is best. Anne, dearest child, women were meant to obey and be protected. You know this."

Charlotte watched the two and wondered what God and the stars had ordained for them. She pressed a small ruby ring into Anne's hand. "You'll be in my prayers."

"Thank you, Madame." Anne understood she had

alerted everyone to her dismay. She'd be given no chance to escape even if she risked the peril of the cross. Yet the Queen meant well. She smiled dully. "You are kind, Madame."

"May the saints and Blessed Virgin watch over you." Charlotte thought it sad to see a young girl so unhappy, but time would bring surcease. It always did.

It was a three day leisurely ride to Amboise. The first night they spent at the adorned fortress, Saumer, where gilt weathervanes glittered on a forest of slim towers. By the second stop at Plessis-les-Tours, the dark and grim castle which was Louis's favourite residence, the two waiting-women, Dames Agnes and Valerie, assigned to the Nevilles by Charlotte, whimpered they were stiff with saddle-sores. Their delicate bodies weren't accustomed to such an indelicate condition. Anne wanted to laugh. They'd not get far in Yorkshire.

The third day they approached Amboise where the château of old stone brooded darkly on high ground over the clutter of huts below. Anne saw the Prince riding toward them. She let herself imagine for a moment this was another place, another person.

" 'Tis His Grace," one of the attendants hissed. "We're honoured."

The countess moved to her daughter's side. "Anne, don't harden your heart. It will only bring grief."

Edward of Lancaster lifted his cap, smiled. "Countess, Lady Anne, all of you, welcome." His eyes roamed over Anne thoughtfully. His bride. In countless dreams, in myriad ways, he'd possessed her. Soon dreams would be reality.

Anne wet dry lips. "It's gracious of you to ride out and meet us." In the clear daylight his smile had the Valois thinness. Cool arrogant eyes were from his mother's side.

Edward moved his horse alongside the girl's as they rode upward toward the château. "*Tu es vraiment belle*," he whispered. "I thought a marriage of politics meant a long-nosed bride with bad teeth. The English all have rotted teeth." Heat filled his loins. He wanted her. Immediately, as he always wanted. She seemed to have grown in the single week.

"I think England will have many pleasant surprises for you." Her voice was neutral.

"After nine years in exile, God's nails, it should."

He drew closer, his thigh pressed against her. "My mother hates you." His left arm crept about her waist. "But, by Venus, we can find better things to do than hate." He wanted to rip away the thin silk of her bodice.

His arm was tight, hot. Anne could hear the ladies' soft tittering.

"When we know each other better ..." Anne couldn't finish. Every night with this man would be rape, she thought. Every part of her body his plaything. He had waited nine years to revenge himself on York. Her blood would be the first.

His hand moved across her bodice, cupped her breast. "Such a pleasure to know everything about you. Soon."

She couldn't answer and he laughed.

At the top of the incline, where a straggly border garden and broken walls marked the château grounds, Margaret greeted them.

Anne jumped off her horse, stumbled in the absence of a mounting-block, but managed to turn it into a curtsy.

Margaret stood with lips drawn back. "So you came." She waved a hand. "Amboise. The ends of the earth. The animals here are better-kept than humans." Margaret thought of the prize horses and falcons. They'd better quarters than the small, dank room she planned for the countess and this girl. Even Margaret could see Anne looked fresher, less tired, more mature. She realized the women in attendance meant Queen Charlotte had taken an interest in the bawd. Margaret's torturing compromise engulfed her. "God's death, that we ally ourselves with the Nevilles."

Anne walked slowly to the main door of the château. A slight breeze pulled at her hair and skirts in the early-evening coolness. She watched her mother avoid Margaret as though the Queen did not exist.

"Come, Anne, let's go in. This day is almost over. Soon another will go by." She put her arm around Anne's shoulders. "And I'll stay with you."

The days would go by, slowly, relentlessly, until all was resolved. Until her father conquered England and she married and Richard died. Or perhaps other futures would come. All days finally ended in death. She saw Edward watching her and turned into the château. She couldn't bear to think of any future. No matter how the way twisted, she'd vowed to marry Edward.

IV

Richard, Earl of Warwick, glared at Louis's messanger. He was at the end of his temper. "You don't understand," he told Jean Bourré. "The Burgundian fleet hampers my every move. They control the Norman coast. How am I to sail to England?"

Bourré pulled out a bag of coins. "Pay your men. I hear they're anxious."

"They've too much time to think." Warwick didn't add he knew they feared a hangman's noose would greet them in England. Many were more pirate than fighter. "Tell King Louis to attack Burgundy. Duke Charles is his vassal."

"King Louis is bound by the treaty of Peronne. He'd be foolish to break it, until you control England. Burgundy is a great power. Louis is never foolish." Bourré watched the earl. The man looked older than he'd anticipated. But Louis had ordered that the earl be paid what he needed. Bourré and his colleague, Tanguy du Chastrel, knew the King was a thrifty man. And he expected absolute obedience.

Warwick counted out the coins. It was enough, just enough. Humiliating. To beg. His banquets, his estates, his style, had outshown all kings. The gall had a bitter taste, but he had to swallow. He wrote to his countess that, God willing, the blockade would break and he would sail.

Anne read the letter and wondered what her father felt under the façade of impenetrable greatness, or perhaps the bravura surface was now his entire being.

"Isn't Charles of Burgundy married to King Edward's sister?" She remembered hearing Clarence speak of his youngest sister Margaret and her brilliant match with the famous duke.

"Charles the Bold. The Rash. Yes, so today he's England's ally. Besides he hates being a vassal to Louis. 'Tis said his knees creak when he bends them."

Anne laughed. The letter had been a small diversion in the boredom of long pointless days. The room was small, mice scurried at night, spiders claimed and reclaimed large corners. Large, black roaches hid in the bedclothes. The slight breeze of August brushed by the narrow window leaving unchanged the stale air, old with decay and mildew. The women assigned to them by Charlotte gave grudging service. Margaret kept to her own room. Edward rode out daily. Even meals were sent up on a tray. The wine had gone sour in the heat of summer. Anne stretched. Her young legs felt cramped. She wished she could take a horse and ride and never come back.

From the window she could just see one section of the garden which was attended. Neat borders, a thick trimmed hedge. She couldn't see a gardener.

Her mother sat on the coffer which contained their clothes, holding the rosary she'd always used. The coral beads were motionless in her fingers. She seemed to be waiting.

"May I go out to the garden?" Anne felt foolish bothering her mother with such a small matter. At home she'd raced about even, up to a few years ago, standing with the sentinels, bravely watching the horizon.

"Of course, Anne. It's dull for you. For me. But I've learned to wait. I can sit here and think of your father."

"And pray for him?"

"Yes."

"And for a great triumph?"

"Just for him, Anne. Everything else follows." The countess forced a smile. Her child was turning into a woman with each passing day.

In the garden the girl contemplated the neglected, brown plants. To her all France was an arid desolation like this. She strolled over to the one colourful patch, puzzled. This section had a touch of England in spite of the hot sun and dry wind. Keeping himself carefully in the shade of the high hedge, an elderly gentleman, wearing a côte-hardie, stylish a generation before, pruned a border of marigolds.

He saw her. Made a spry bow. "Would you care for some flowers, Lady Anne? Any you wish."

The crown of his head was burned a deep tan within the circle of a grey fringe of hair. His small brown eyes were shrewd but kind. "St Adelard is with me. My garden flourishes even here."

"But you're not a gardener, sir?"

He laughed. "I'm Sir John Fortescue, lawyer, English, and tutor to Prince Edward."

Fortescue was known for his political acumen, even to Anne. She wondered how he had ended on the Lancastrian side. No doubt his horoscope would explain. "I'd like a bouquet." She smiled uncertainly at him. "Our room is very drab."

"Everything is drab here. Until recently, but then you know all about that, there were not two pennies to rub together among the lot of us." His voice was amiable and without bitterness. "So I took a small corner of the grounds for my own. After all, I must do something with my time. The Prince doesn't care to linger at his studies." Eyes squinted against the sun, he studied her. *Une belle jeune fille.* Even in plaits, her hair full of light fell like bell-ropes below her waist. He saw the sadness in her large grey-blue eyes. A proud little thing, he would guess.

"Edward, the Prince, knows the ways of England? He'll be a worthy ruler?" Anne sensed she dared ask this man anything.

Sir John nodded slowly. "The Prince is intelligent. Not at all like his poor addled father. The Valois line is strong. And with these years in France ... Of course, he needs to be about a man's business. This life is not good for a young man. Strong emotion and appetites go unslaked here."

"He should go to England then."

"Ah, Lady Anne, Queen Margaret would not risk him until your father has secured England. Then, too," he smiled, "there is the matter of your wedding."

"Yes, of course." Anne sat down in the grass along the carefully tended flower border. "Perhaps the Queen will postpone it. I'm sure she'd like to."

"And you're in no hurry?"

Anne picked a golden flower and tucked it in the neckline of her dress. "Sir John, I would be glad if this wedding were delayed until I am old and ugly and Edward would have none of me." She leaned back, lifting her face to the sun. "Perhaps, if I cut my hair, very short."

"You feel nothing for the Prince?" Fortescue was surprised. He knew the boy was handsome. This lovely girl was a perfect mate. Such beauty could gentle even Edward of Lancaster. Satisfy his lust.

"I don't know him. The Queen hates me."

"Yes, she has said as much. Yet I think she recognizes

the inevitability of this match. She wants no grandchildren."

"She'll forbid Edward to consummate the marriage?" Anne's eyes opened wide. She had not dared hope for such a boon.

Fortescue shook his head. "No, child. You're the reason the Prince is content to stay. I hope you don't conceive. The Prince is a virile man."

"She'll kill me, or make me to take a drug to abort a child. If there is a child." Anne thought of Isabel. In her mind a fully formed babe lay dead in her arms.

"No. No." Fortescue had seen the white agony on Anne's face. "We will be in England by such time. Everything will be different. You must not be afraid. Surely you know all will be well in England." He patted her lightly on the head. "Your father is a great man. I know little of military matters. I know I haven't seen England in nine years. I'll be glad to go home."

He bent over and picked a few daisies. "These were the symbol of Margaret of Anjou when she first came to London. Did you know? So, you see, I grow daisies. But they also flourish in England. Pick all you want. And someday soon I'll brag how an old man gave flowers to a beautiful young Princess."

"You're not old, Sir John."

"My dear, anyone who has lived in the household of Margaret of Anjou for nine years is very, very old." He glanced uneasily toward the tower rooms. "And now I must attend her. Every day we discuss the return to England. Please linger if this small place pleases you. The air is sweet this time of day."

Anne spread her skirts out. "Thank you. May I come again?"

"Of course, as often as you like. No one else ever does.

Next time perhaps you might be so kind as to tell me how it is in England. It couldn't be as lovely as I remember." He was gone with a polite bow.

She closed her eyes. The air was fresh. John Fortescue was a friend in a way. The Queen wanted no grandchildren. Let her then keep the Prince with the village sluts. Perhaps there might be a way through this long maze.

"Well, little bird, you fly about all aone."

Anne jumped up. "I didn't see you."

"You don't seek very hard for me, *ma belle*. Edward held a riding-crop in one hand. He felt flushed and tall in his riding-boots. The girl wanted to run. He could tell. Resistance always aroused him. Fortescue had called him a 'tomcat' only yesterday.

"I was talking to Sir John," Anne said nervously. "He's a pleasant man."

Edward shrugged and moved closer. "Sir John and his pleasantries bored me when I was ten. A stinking swamp of fine words. I'm buried alive in 'maybes' and 'have patiences'."

"Yes, I suppose so." She thought, without finding comfort in it, that he did have the Plantagenet easy confidence. But then she and half the royalty in England were all descended from Edward III. Both Yorkist and Lancastrian. Now time had come again for the Lancastrians.

"No doubt, you'll see much fighting yet," she said slowly. "Though I hope not." She edged toward the château. She had to get away.

"Women always want peace, except my mother. You're not at all like her, *mon amie*." Edward stepped nearer, blocking her retreat. "The cook has just sent a stuffed capon and a bottle of wine to my room. Come, join me. Add savour to my meal."

"It wouldn't be proper." The words sounded foolish. "I'm not hungry." Her heart had begun thumping like a chased rabbit. She drew her skirts about, trying to pass him.

"Anne. You're young. I'm young." He caught her by the arm. "I promise you such pleasure." His free hand caressed her breast, soft beneath silk. "Little filly, you want this." He pulled her closer, his other hand a band of steel on her wrist.

"No. Please. No. When I'm your wife, well, I'll do my duty." She had to stay calm. He'd probably relish a struggle. His hand rubbed against her tender flesh. She knew this was the way of lovers. Isabel had told her. But his caresses hurt and shamed. "Are you a Prince or debaucher?" Anne held to her own pride. Let him see himself as base.

Edward laughed. "Sweet innocence. I must teach you." He drew her against him, forced her lips open under the hard pressure of his kiss.

Anne jerked her face aside and stumbled back into the garden, crushing the flowers. "I'm your bride, not your slut." She backed away, her eyes bright with anger. "Find someone else until we're married."

The Prince watched in amazement. A little tiger kitten, he'd not suspected. The chronic boredom lessened. "All this for sampling the goods – with only my hand – before I claim them." His words mocked. Do you know how dreary life is here? I've read every book in Amboise, ridden all the trails, drunk every wine. I can barely remember England. We've been here forever. You must amuse me before I die of dullness.

"Soon you'll be in England." Anne watched him, trying slowly to edge toward the château. She was well aware the hedge hid them. "You'll like England. The country is so green. And rich."

"Will the people cheer me?"

"Yes. You'll wave. The fortune in the Tower will be yours someday, after my father wins for Lancaster." She stopped. The Yorkists would be dead. She closed her eyes against the pain. If only she could stop thinking.

In that moment Edward seized her. He kissed her and wondered if he should let her go after all. She was delightful. God, her skin was soft and scented. He'd never before known anyone who smelled of flowers. How easy it would be to take her, rip her maidenhood, shed York blood. Tempting. Someday, as a lusty woman, she'd marvel at his restraint. He realized talking with her had increased his desire. This was no kitchen wench. They were betrothed. He pulled her down, crushing her beneath him. She twisted and fought. Edward was elated. There'd be no boredom in her wedding-bed.

"The wedding-night." Anne's voice was a hoarse whisper. "You deserve a virgin."

Edward stared down at her. Damnation. She was right. He was a Prince. He drew back and looked at her with braids loosened, her little body not fully ripe and her lips flecked with blood where his teeth had cut. "The marriage bed. You promise good sport?"

Her words came in pent breaths. "Edward, I'll do anything you want, as your wife. Isn't that worth a short wait?"

"You'll do anything I want as my wife anyway."

Tears ran down her cheeks, so she tasted salt with blood. "I mean a willing wife, not forced."

"Anne, you persuade me." Abruptly Edward released her. He watched as she covered herself, pulling her long hair over the rips in the fragile silk gown. No reason to tell her he'd never planned more than a romp anyway. He'd found what he wanted, a lovely, innocent body and a hot-blooded minx. "As I said, we're both young. A time for pleasure." He pulled a cluster of Fortescue's flowers and handed them to her. "A token of all the gifts I'll give you someday."

"Edward, just be gentle with me." Anne slowly got up. Her back felt bruised. Dust and plant stains smeared her skirts.

"Gentle? No." He was beside her, taller by a foot. "I refuse to have a tedious marriage. The Prince and Princess of England can't be a sluggish pair. I'll teach you many tricks. You'll see."

Anne nodded. He exists for self-gratification, she realized in distress, and arrogance controls very action. She could be thankful for his conceit; it had protected her today.

She clasped the drooping flowers and began walking toward the château. With luck her mother would be napping and she'd see no one.

Edward strolled beside her, whistling.

V

Warwick gave thanks to St George. An autumn storm had broken the blockade. Shortly the fleet would land at Dartmouth and Plymouth. His natural optimism ruled. The sailors' cheers echoed in his mind. He was eager to unite with his brother John. True, John Neville had been maddeningly loyal to King Edward, but those were the days when John was Duke of Northumberland. Now Edward had snatched the dukedom away and returned it to the Percies. The Nevilles and Percies had always competed for the north. And it was a double insult to give John the meaningless title of Marquess of Montagu. Surely now he would fight with his own brother, his own blood. He was almost thirty-eight, old enough by far to understand the compromises necessary in life. Warwick remembered suddenly that John was Anne's favourite uncle. He wondered briefly how she fared.

On September 13 the gangplank thudded down in England. The townsmen stayed inside. No one offered resistance. Warwick learned the King was in the north surpressing the local rebillion, caused by Lancastrian agents. A message caught up with him from Louis assuring him of continued support. The French King had made

offerings and prayers both at St Gatien Cathedral and
Notre Dame de la Délivrance. Warwick was still smiling as
he organized his men to move northeastward toward
London. Louis left nothing to chance. He'd managed to see
God blessed the right side.

In Northumberland John Neville agonized. *Traitor.* The
word pained his heart. Attack Edward? He might win. Kill
Edward? Impossible. He summoned his son George, a
skinny boy of twelve.

"If I march against the King, what will you think of me?
My forces outnumber the royal ones."

"But you don't want to.". It was a statement, not a
question.

"Edward forfeited my allegiance." John covered his face
with his hands. He hadn't wept in years. Tears scalded his
eyes and he blinked them back. He must decide.

His son said slowly, "If you stay with the King, you'll
have to fight your own brother."

"And be damned as Cain." John stood, suddenly an old
man. "God forgive us all." Empty words. He found no
comfort in them.

Warwick received his brother's letter. The earl felt
triumph in his bones. John was finally with him. He
remembered the first victory at St Albans. He'd been
twenty-six. The glory of winning never diminished.

Soon other allies joined the Warwick-Lancastrian
numbers. The Earl of Shrewsbury and Lord Stanley
brought several thousand men. Louis's prayers were being
heard. Better yet, John Neville started south with a force
strong enough to crush Edward's army.

A surfeit of good news followed. Edward and a small
band of followers had run. Had barely gotten away with
their skins. They'd slipped to the coast and sailed from
Lynn. The waters were rough there. They had only small

craft. Warwick hoped the Channel would claim them. He knew things seldom worked out so neatly – and easily. Perhaps this one time. Now, the first week in October he pressed for London.

At Amboise Anne read hasty, joyful letters her father wrote to his wife. He never mentioned his daughter. He described at some length John's defection from the King. A sign Heaven blessed his Enterprise.

"Uncle John is the soul of consistency," Anne was puzzled.

"Family ties are strong." The countess reached for the letter. She read each one over and over. Her husband did the impossible. She'd come to accept any expediency, any compromise for his sake.

"What do you think will happen, mama?"

The countess shook her head. "I can only pray."

Anne glanced at the coral rosary which entwined her mother's fingers. "For what do you pray?"

Anne Beauchamp regarded her daughter in faint surprise. "Why, for salvation. May we all know grace. I fear your Uncle John is sore at heart. I pray he'll find ease and be worthy of my lord husband."

"You don't ask for our estates restored? For victory?"

"Oh, aye, for many worldly things." The beads slipped slackly through her fingers. "God has promised us nothing in this world, only in the next."

"Yes, but ..." Anne thought her mother looked very old this autumn. It was as if ten years had passed. The indentations about her mouth cut deeper. Grey streaked her hair.

The countess gazed into the far distance. "When you're older, Anne, you won't ask such questions of me or of God." She felt pity for the girl. Being Princess of Wales wouldn't assure happiness. But, then, how rare was happiness! Perhaps the most scarce of earth's treasures. At Westminster someday Anne would at least be secure.

During the next weeks messangers began to arrive regularly from King Louis. The Lancastrian advance moved unchallenged toward London. Warwick led them openly with John de Vere by his side. Many Kentishmen flocked to the Lancastrian standard.

Sir John Fortescue suggested wine to celebrate and insisted Edward and Anne join him. He had never mentioned his crushed garden. Over the wine he said casually, "I've been learning cards. I hear they're all the fad in England. Let me teach you a game?"

Edward hooked his fingers in his belt. He liked the idea of something fashionable. "I'd find it amusing."

"And you, Lady Anne?" Sir John's round face pleaded. The girl had lost her flush of summer sun. He thought she looked ill.

"Of course." Anne was dimly aware Sir John was trying to help. She pushed her fears into the back of her mind. Her life had been too sheltered, too perfect until last April. Still this was no excuse for weakness.

Edward dealt the cards easily. "Sir John swears we'll like this better than backgammon. Do we wager?"

"Oh, pennies, if you wish." Fortescue leaned back in the window seat so Edward and Anne were directly across a small table from each other.

She tried to smile. "I've no pennies."

"Kisses?" Edward said it lightly.

"A lock of my hair, if you win."

"Done." Edward began to assort his cards. "I doubt Sir John will hold you to such a bargain, but I will, Anne."

They began to play, a simple game, hearts were high.

Fortescue threw away points. Sometimes to Anne, more often to Edward.

The score grew. Edward looked at his cards and grinned. "Anne, tell me about the battles you've seen."

"Why, none. Women do not ..." She stopped. His mother had led armies.

"Well, then, heard about."

"I was no more than a baby when some were fought." The cards blurred in front of her. It was true. During much of her calm life, civil war had raged in England. Her father had never let it touch his family. "I remember names. Northampton. Mortimer's Cross. Sometime later at a place called Hedgley Moor my Uncle John slew Sir Ralph Percy. And became Duke of Northumberland till it was taken from him." Anne didn't hear the anger in her voice. She thought of Uncle John. He had called her his golden butterfly. "Of course, I remember the second St Albans." People still talked of it. So many had died. Margaret had ravaged the countryside. Even commoners, who cared for no political quarrel, had been murdered in the heat of the struggle. The Queen had won, but London had refused to admit her afterwards.

Edward nodded. "My mother says the whole bloody mess was all due to the Yorkists. After they captured my father at the first St Albans she turned into a lioness. My father and I were cubs."

Anne regarded him uneasily. "Your father was captured by chance," she said tactfully.

"Oh, I know the story. They found him sitting under an oak, singing. He studied his cards for a moment. "It will be different when I command. My father prayed and the victories bounced back and forth. I plan to use cannon."

"Everyone uses cannons now. It's tricky not to overshoot.

Some say." Anne felt lost in the conversation. She'd heard cannons exploded unless perfectly cast, but decided not to mention it.

Edward laughed and slapped down a card. "King Louis and his engineers know more about cannons than anyone else. I'll learn from them. How my enemies will run, if any are left alive. I think you owe me a lock of hair, Anne."

"Yes." She held out one of her braids and he easily cut a small curling end with a tiny Italian-style poniard. He stood for a moment staring at the wisp of curl in the palm of his hand. He had never felt real tenderness toward anything. The strange emotion bothered him. He didn't recognize it, except as new and weak. He had never to be weak.

"You have beautiful hair, Anne. It shines. Why don't you wear it loose?" He was amazed at his own words.

"I will, if you like," she said slowly.

John Fortescue beamed. Long observation of people and life gave him more understanding than either of the two youngsters. The gentling had begun. "Lady Anne, you must teach the Prince here some of the courtly dances. He has never learned them."

Edward laughed. "I don't intend to dance, Fortescue. I know how to kill. De Vere told me often the way of it. So easy. To plunge a sword into a man. It's like stabbing a pillow." He glanced at Anne, wondering if she was impressed.

"And afterwards, at court, you will celebrate — and dance." Sir John said mildly.

"Everyone does. We all learned ... once." Anne couldn't say the word 'Middleham' here."

"Does the Yorkist King dance?" Edward looked amazed.

"Every evening. So I've heard." Anne thought of the tall giant tripping about on the dance-floor. Yet she'd also heard he was graceful as a young god.

"Well, then," the Prince shrugged. "You must teach me, Anne."

And so she did under the benevolent eye of John Fortescue. They practiced dance-steps, compared astrological signs, played chess. Anne hoped that somewhere their minds would meet and they could be friends. Through the shortening, chill days of autumn she searched for such a bedrock. Edward dreamed only of battle, of dead enemies and glory. She didn't want to think of that battle or those dead. Her inner desperation deepened. This man would own her body. She had pledged on the true cross. How could it be then her marriage loomed a thing of cynicism and suffering? Surely God would forbid it.

In Bruges, a threadbare guest of Seigneur Gruthuyse, Governor of Holland, Richard of Gloucester wondered if there was anything God forbade. He and his brother and a few men had barely made it to shore and safety. Twice the Channel had beaten back their tiny fleet while the ships had almost floundered and taken on water. Finally, vessels of the Easterlings had chased them to the beaches of Alkmaar where Gruthuyse had rescued them. Now they lived on his charity and hoped their brother-in-law Charles of Burgundy would see fit to support a military return. Richard was not used to having nothing to do. He skated on the frozen river Reye, the bone skates clacking. He found himself frequently alone. The other men with Edward of York had made themselves comfortable. The ladies of Bruges were amiable; time was in surplus. Charles hinted he might receive them after Christmas. It was a busy season just now. Richard imagined how busy it must be for Warwick in London. The busyness of triumph. England lost because Edward was lazy. Gulled. He trusted too easily, as they all did. Trusted until the knife drew blood. They'd honestly believed the rebellion in Yorkshire was a local matter, not the diversion it had proven. Even as they ran like mice, Edward puzzled over John Neville's desertion.

And now they waited. Richard divided his time between Gruthuyse's fine house and the port of Flushing. There the fleet was to assemble which would carry them back to England. Richard often sat on the cold docks and watched the cranes, small by London standards. Over and over in his mind he heard Edward say, "You were right. By the Devil's tail, the little Anne is to marry the Lancastrian."

He had asked what the Prince was like and Edward had shrugged. "A braggart and out for blood, so I've heard. I wouldn't have thought Warwick would sink so low in the final pinch."

In his heart neither had Richard. He thought of the distance to Anne. Not so great in miles. Yet it might as well be the stars. He stared down into the filthy grey water. Chunks of ice bumped against the dock. The men working the cranes shouted to each other, their voices hoarse with cold.

If only he had married her even when she was a child. Consummation could have come later. He could have protected her. Sheltered her. The wind bit through his own wool-lined cloak, the borrowed beaver hat, the padded doublet. He couldn't protect even himself.

He began walking back from the pier his steps quickening, so his clogs banged. The pale sunlight began to fade. Now Edward asked him to go to their sister in Burgundy and somehow work a miracle. Tomorrow he'd leave for Lille.

A day later in the splendour of the Burgundian palace,

Richard greeted his sister. She danced toward him a swirl of velvets, ermine and jewels. "You look lovely, Maggie," he said truthfully.

"And you look a bit shabby, Dick. Can't a tailor fix that doublet? It's too big."

"And only for short-term use." He was impatient with these amenities, but women would chat. There was no getting round it. A half hour later he mentioned Fotheringhay.

"Mother's still there?" Maggie was choosing veils to go with her new, towering headdress.

"Yes, we hope. Remember when we were children at Fotheringhay, you and I and George? We both adored you."

"And still do, I trust."

"Edward and I worry about George. He's in a thorny maze. He was foolish to go with Warwick, but then a man in love ... Isabel Neville's a pretty lass."

"He'd return to York?"

"With a little help, a reminder from an adored sister of the fondness we all share for him."

"The prodigal," Maggie laughed. "You'll have to kill a fatted calf."

"But you'll help persuade him?"

"Aye. I'm already in touch with George. I'll tell him about your fatted calf named Warwick." She laughed and Richard joined her though he felt his face would crack.

VI

King Louis of France spread his hands and a giant ruby flashed. Nothing else bespoke a King. He had just arrived from Tours and his drab clothes were grimy, his hair windblown, several new lead medals weighed his cap. He'd gathered them all in the damp centre hall at Amboise, kissed Margaret. The black-beetles scurried to hide. Tinder tried feebly to ignite a log on the old-style central hearth.

"*Chère cousine,*" Louis spoke in a rush, "your husband has been released from the Tower, once again he's King of England. You're Queen in every sense of the word." His curiously charming smile above the slab of a jaw shifted to Edward. "And you're Prince of Wales. How does it feel to be resurrected?"

"Justice has prevailed." Margaret crossed herself. "But the Yorkists? What of them?"

Louis shrugged. "They escaped, to Holland, unfortunately. Still, I hear they are penniless. A poor man has no friends. The Yorkists in London are in sanctuaries. The Woodville woman, no longer Queen, is in the sanctuary of Westminster where she awaits a most inopportune child England is won!"

"George, Duke of Clarence?" The countess asked quietly, but her eyes were intent.

Louis looked surprised. "I'd forgotten about him. I believe he's staying at The Erber which, am I not right, was once the home of your father-in-law? The Earl of Warwick, of course, stays with the King at the Bishop of London's palace."

"Isabel should join her husband." Anne Beauchamp was firm. "He needs her."

Louis nodded smoothly. "Then the Lady Isabel will soon sail for England. It's well to remind the duke his allegiance is with Warwick." He suddenly remembered what Charlotte had told him after meeting with the countess and her daughter. They could no more be trusted than the false summer which sometimes came in March. He was glad he had no son-in-law. Or a wilful daughter.

"But the Yorkists will attempt to return? There will be battles yet?" The Prince spoke from behind Anne. His voice eager as though he asked about a festive hunt.

"Oh, most likely." Louis's generous smile included all. "And you, *mon* Prince, will fight gloriously." He motioned them to draw closer. "In the meantime let us plan the happy business of your wedding and triumphant return to London." He concentrated on Anne. "Damoiselle, I'd give all the medals off my cap to be young as your Prince and be your bridegroom." He judged her pale, thinner. Charlotte had expressed great fondness for this girl. He though she was more unhappy and confused than she'd admit even to herself. She was *une brave*.

Anne glanced at Edward. She knew now his warfare talk was no pose. He'd been waiting nine dull years while he grew sure he would someday kill all his enemies in bloody triumph without mercy. Soon they would be joined together, one in the sight of God and men. Desperation made her daring. "Couldn't we postpone the wedding?" She heard the collective gasp. "I might conceive. It would be difficult." Her heart was beating as though it would break through her chest.

"I'll see you don't conceive, Neville." Margaret's voice grated. The thought was unbearable, her son's union with this spawn of Warwick's. She remembered she'd planned to use Anne to keep Edward contented. Passion cancelled reason. Somehow she would persuade her son not to go to his bride.

Louis laughed. "Ah, you wish to argue what has been settled. Come, we're all in this venture. Marriage was promised. A simple ceremony but binding 'fore God. I believe a man has a right to his wife's bed." He put a paternal arm about Edward. "I'll loan the state sword for the day. A splendid thing. Afterwards ride her high, boy. She'll like that."

"And often." Edward grinned back. He felt a man of the world.

Louis doffed his cap. "God and Saint Barbara have heard all our prayers. I'm giving a great taper and six vessels of silver to Notre Dame de la Délivrance, plus my own image in wax. All will arrange itself. One of my merchants in Tours will supply samples from which you may choose a fabric for your wedding-gown, Lady Anne. *Au revoir. Dieu vous garde.* Yuletide nuptials perhaps. Charlotte sends her love ..." He was out the door still talking.

The countess sat down abruptly. "My husband rules in London again. God protect him."

"It's Henry VI who rules," Margaret glared.

"Mother, we all know how things stand." Edward took her arm. "There are still victories to be won. We mustn't divide ourselves."

A Plantagenet would speak so, Anne thought sadly. If only he had been raised to want something beside conquests and revenge. If only there was a little balance in him. Soon they would share a marriage bed. That, too, would represent a conquest. She was sure the Prince believed he had striven most patiently to make her surrender in gladness. She wondered bleakly what he would demand.

Edward, surrounded again by three women, smothered in his mother's concern, thought of his sword. So bright a blade. Soon he would stain it with blood. He felt exorbitant anticipation. Battle. But first he had to ride his bride high.

Louis, prodded by Charlotte, did his best. A prosperous merchant in Tours, Jean de Beaune, greased the sluggish wheels of Church machinery to facilitate a dispensation, necessary since Edward and Anne were second cousins. Another merchant, Jean Briconnet, sent samples of silks, linen, velvet and cloth of gold from his own collection to the bride as well as the countess and Margaret. They could choose whatever they fancied. News from London came frequently. Parliament accepted Warwick's government. Edward of York was declared a usurper and he and Richard of Gloucester put under attainder. Other Yorkists were allowed to keep their estates. In sanctuary, former Queen Elizabeth Woodville gave birth to a son.

Alone, holding her full skirts tightly about her for warmth, the tight sleeves of her woollen gown itching against her arms, her toes curled against the cold, Anne counted those who had to die if, in the end, her father won. Edward of York, Richard, perhaps Isabel's George, and now this baby. She thought of Richard lying in a field of green, his face white from lost blood, a dagger-wound in his throat. A merciful death, many would say. The image haunted her dreams. She willed him to live in her night's imaginings and sometimes he did, but always in the past. At Middleham, children, learning Latin and sums and laughing at their tutor. Once she dreamed of the last time at Warwick, the moment of declared love. But always the dream of death returned and each time his body was more mutilated, more diminished against the green. She knew she could share her pain with no one. Even her mother would dismiss dreams.

The second week in December the dispensation arrived, granted by Louis de Harcourt, Patriarch of Jerusalem. The dresses were quickly finished then, the château swept and cleaned. Sandalwood candles scented the air. Festive logs, wrapped in flames of orange and green, burned in the main Hall. On the evening of December 12 an elaborate dinner was served.

Platters of food steamed out from the kitchen. A juggler jumped about while merrily keeping aloft six silver-gilt balls. Minstrels sang tender love-ballads. The aroma of cinnamon and cloves hung heavily in the air. The Counts of Eu and Vendome and the Lord of Chatillon came dressed in rich velvets and furs. They were the guard of honour to escort them to Paris later in the week. Anne saw them eat with relish and wondered how many of Louis's gold écus paid for this winter venture.

Edward, next to his bride at the high table, whispered in her ear, "You're beautiful, *mon amie*. I'll kiss your eyes tomorrow. They're blue as your dress. I'll kiss each part of you. Little bird, *je t'aime*." Hidden by the table he caressed her thighs. Anne tried to smile. She didn't want to anger him.

She had become so thin, Edward thought. He could take her standing. The idea had possibilities. Lifting her on his erection he could penetrate deeply. Yet there'd be no sense of submission. He'd save it for later. He briefly pondered all the many ways of sex, the orifices he could claim. No. The *virgo intacta* had to be his first act. He hoped she'd bleed.

Stained sheets were a sign of success.

The Count of Vendome, unaware no one listened, finished a long dissertation on vineyards and soil conditions.

"But yes, Monsieur," Anne answered automatically, "the wine here in the Loire valley is exceptional."

"Ah, Mademoiselle." Vendome motioned a page forward to again fill his cup. Dark tuffed hair stood upright on his ringed hands. His nails were black and jagged. "There are many specialities in this area. Shad and pike from the river, goat's-milk cheese, mushrooms ..." He belched and licked his lips.

"And men," grinned the Count of Eu. He adjusted the chain about his shoulders. "French men. Your Prince has the best of both countries."

Anne stared down the length of the Hall. She'd been in this dismal place since August. Tomorrow she'd be married. The day after they'd leave for Paris. Then England.

She knew her mother watched her anxiously and Anne fancied she could see herself reflected in those worried eyes. When she left Amboise she would be Princess of Wales. She wondered if her mother had prayed for that.

At a side-table John Fortescue watched and hoped he had helped. Edward was not cruel. He simply was trained by his mother from the cradle. Sir John knew he had never dented the fixed resolve of the Prince, not even as a lad. He hoped Anne Neville would bring the change, show the Prince life was not just for killing. He knew it was probably too late. The Prince had been set on his course so long ago.

Margaret looked at no one. She had accepted none of Louis's fabrics. Tomorrow was a time of mourning. Her undisciplined rage burned higher than the night of the fire. Someday she'd kill the slut who dared marry her son. It was the only thought which brought comfort.

Later, in the night, long after the last of the candles had been put out and the guests of King Louis retired to newly freshened chambers, Anne knelt at the plain prie-dieu of the solar which she shared this last night with her mother. She didn't pray. "I'll not judge anyone," she explained to a remote creator. "Everyone says what my father has done is right and wonderful. I don't think so, but he is my father. I'll marry, for I promised. Sometimes I've wanted to break that pledge. Even if I died. But I can't. Perhaps I'm an idealistic fool. Perhaps I should learn corruption." She shuddered and was silent. She was indeed a fool to think God would listen to such nonsense. "I'll marry," she whispered again. "Then go to England." Anne shifted on her knees. "And I'll be strong. Perhaps I can protect Richard, my love who should have been my life." The girl bowed her head against the railing. "Tomorrow a part of me will die."

VII

December 13 dawned, shrouded in grey. Rain spattered. Low clouds wrapped damp wisps of fog about the château. It didn't matter. The marriage was to take place in the small, private chapel at Amboise. Louis had indeed been as good as his word in suggesting the ceremony be unpretentious. His support of Warwick and the Lancastrians had cost him dearly. He had dispatched a decorative jewelled sword for Edward to wear for the occasion, a loan of course. Charlotte had sent her favourite tiring-woman, Elinore de Millay, to attend the bride, also a loan.

Under Elinor's guidance Anne stood in the centre of the group of three chattering women who bathed and dressed her. Dames Agnes and Valerie were happy. Their long exile from court would soon be over. Elinore worked as one who knows what must be done. In silence Anne raised her arms, turned, tilted her head and wondered they could not all hear the slow beating of her heart.

Dame Elinore slipped the linen shift about the girl and deftly arranged the soft wool hose. "You're going to be a lovely bride, Lady Anne. Such hair, so long."

Anne thanked her.

"A pity it's raining." Dame Valerie lifted the wedding-gown down from its perch. "*Diable à quartre*, I don't like evil omens."

"Never mind, *ma petite Damoiselle*." Dame Elinore adjusted the high waistline of the dress. "You're as fair as the fairest skies."

Dame Agnes shrugged. "Why fret about rain? 'Tis the tumble in bed afterwards that matters."

"Aye." Elinore glanced at the bride, then smiled at Agnes and said in honeyed tones. "The Prince won't be dry as tinder as your old man must be, my dame."

Valerie giggled. Even the countess, sitting and watching, smiled. Elinore was known for her curt tongue toward all except Charlotte.

Staring down at the billowing skirts about her, Anne heard little of the talk. The gown was a rich tone of blue-green known as angel's eye velvet. Silk and velvet cinctures at the waist were trimmed with ermine. It was a beautiful dress. The thought flickered through her mind like a stinging lash; no, it was a beautiful winding-sheet.

Elinore gently patted the girl's cheek. "Mademoiselle, I'm clever with paste and paint. Let me put a bit of colour on your cheeks and eyes."

Anne shook her head.

"Perhaps you'd like some hot chocolate and fresh bread? You mustn't faint, you know, my dear." Elinore bit her lips and added slowly. "You've very thin."

The countess rose from the bench. Anne thought her mother looked sad today but not as stricken as when they'd fled Warwick. Well, she was Anne Beauchamp from birth and the inheritance of Warwick was hers. Anne knew quite well it was possible to love a building, a place. Besides this day was no shock; it had been coming for months.

"Anne, dearest child, you should eat. Please, for me."

"Very well, Mama." I will get through this day, Anne vowed. I won't faint or cry. No one will ever know. Except my mother, none care. Isabel liked being married. She giggled and wore perfumes to bed. Women seldom married of their own choosing. She was no different. She could endure.

Her mother took hold of Anne's hand and held it while food was ordered. The other ladies spoke in whispers barely audible above the rain. Anne watched the hour-glass. It was half-full. When the sand reached the centre line, it would be noon.

Noon.

She stood in the doorway of the chapel. The altar's worn surface was covered by a small snatch of velvet. Squat candles burned unevenly, smelling of mutton wax, in brass holders. The Grand Vicar of Bayeux, mitered, vested, croisier blinking with gems, chasuble elegantly draped, waited. A small, twitching acolyte opened a side door and Edward stepped to the altar. Margaret was by his side. The Grand Vicar of Bayeux coughed slightly. Edward turned and looked for his bride.

Margaret watched the girl move slowly down the aisle. She recalled herself at fifteen. She'd been proud. A descendant of Charlemagne through her mother's side. Yet she had felt an amazing, childish pang of homesickness when she'd ridden off to England with the Duke and Duchess of Suffolk, kind though they were, to be a bride in a strange land. She remembered her own shabby marriage in Titchfield Abbey. And the King even then had been more monk than man. Her poor Henry. From the first she'd thought of him as needing protection though he was twenty-four.

Anne was unaware of Margaret or of the small group of onlookers. She stared at the crucifix and the remote plaster

Virgin behind it. Somewhere beyond them she could almost see a green field dotted with wild flowers and a young man who wove clover for her hair. Her steps dragged. She heard the whispered murmur of consternation. Slowly Anne turned and faced Edward.

The Prince took her hand, pulling her to his side. Her skin was like pearls, the incredible, pale gold hair flowed, in sign of virginity, down her back. She seemed unreal. A wood sprite who might vanish.

The Grand Vicar began quickly. The bride appeared faint. The power of Louis XI lurked behind this moment. It was his duty to see all done.

In rapid succession, while the Latin phrases rolled over their heads, the bridal couple knelt, exchanged vows, celebrated the mass and were blessed. It was over. Edward and Anne were man and wife.

She felt Edward helping her up. He bent down and kissed her. She saw Margaret, still in black, the indifferent, bored faces of the others. The rain was coming down harder. Incense vapour hung thickly. Anne placed her fingertips lightly on the back of Edward's hand, in the formal manner, and accepted the congratulations of the guests.

As was proper the ladies robed the bride for the wedding-night in a simple white dressing-gown. Anne's mother fastened the garment about her daughter, tying the traditional love knot in velvet ribbons.

"You're all right?" The countess's fingers were clumsy with anxiety.

"Yes, Mama." Anne knew her paleness had given way to a feverish flush.

Her mother's embrace was trembling, uncertain. "My little one, you were my baby." The countess wiped her tears with her sleeve. For the first time she could not rationalize the dreadful thing she and her husband were doing to Anne. Not with Anne standing there in white, looking beyond hope. It was wrong, wrong from the beginning. She whispered desperately. "Oh, child, be happy."

Anne stared at her and wondered. Did she truly think it possible? "I'll try, Mama."

In the bridal chamber, a fire filled the room with warmth and light. A bottle of wine and two crystal goblets stood on a small table.

Edward, sullen, wrapped in a dressing-gown of dark red, inspected the room critically before he turned to his bride. "Well, the sword's on its way back to Louis." He poured a glass of wine, handed it to her and filled his own. "I vow we'll have a coronation someday, Anne, to make up for this shabby wedding. I'll not be the miser Louis is."

"It doesn't matter, Edward."

"I'll buy you robes of cloth of gold." He drank deeply. "My mother begged me this whole day not to take you to bed. Suddenly she wants the marriage unconsummated. As though I were a monk." He laughed, "Or like my saintly, silly father."

"Your mother perhaps thinks it better to wait." A faint hope stirred in Anne. "She might be right. A child now ..."

"She has forgotten being young." He dismissed his mother's pleading with a wave of his hand. "Fortescue told me I must be courteous, soothing, tender. Tame. A dove. He suggested we dine first and talk."

"I am hungry." Anne smiled. She forced composure, remembering Fortescue's mild and tactful attempts to make this a union of more than simply flesh.

"So drink your wine, wife. I'm done with waiting." Edward hated her poise. He sensed his own need. Eager. Ready.

Anne slowly sipped at the sharp beverage, glowing like

gold in crystal glasses. "We have a lifetime, Edward. Let me tell you again about England. You will ride a white stallion. The children will pelt you with flowers, and fathers will hold up their sons to see you." The wine ran through her empty stomach hotly. The room blurred. The fire burned feverishly against her cheeks.

"We've a lifetime to talk." Edward took the glass from her, brushed back her unbound hair from her face. For the first time since in his early teens he had fumbled his way into a kitchen scullion, he felt unsure. This was his wife.

He kissed her gently remembering Fortescue's numerous cautions. Her lips, warm and moist, tasted of sweetness. "You're mine." The words reassured him. He repeated them in his mind. By God, she was his. No man ever had a fairer bride. He lifted her face so her hair fell about his arms. "Anything I want, remember."

"I remember." She felt remote, beyond fear or hope.

Deftly he undid the bridal knot and pulled the gown from her so she stood naked in his embrace. He stepped back and studied his wife, all the lines of her young body, then turned her slowly, totally around. His own robe was off when she once more faced him. "Come here, Anne."

Slowly, while her numbed mind cried in protest, she walked toward him.

He seized her and pulled her next to his own hard body. The heat of his embrace, the tense dampness of his loins, the possessing violence of his arms and thighs became all her awareness. He forced her to her knees and she thought of the bulls, their eyes wild, giant bodies heaving, as they covered the cows. Animals didn't need love.

She knew how he would take her. It didn't matter. Nothing he did mattered. She would not scream.

When the first light of a grey dawn filled the chamber, he

finally slept. She moved away from him in the large bed and pulled the covers over herself, hiding her anguished body. She felt exhausted, utterly soiled. She dared not cry for it might waken him. Tears would change nothing. He was her husband. She was totally alone. She slept a little in restless exhaustion. When she awoke the sun was fully up and he was bending over her.

"No more," she begged. "Please no more for a little."

He looked at her thoughtfully, then propped himself on his elbow without touching his wife. "You look like a child when you're asleep, Anne."

She didn't answer. Her essential being remained within her violated body. He had claimed no part of that which made her Anne. Hope had perished. She would survive.

VIII

The Christmas season of 1470 wrapped England in a cold, damp fog. From cot to castles people huddled in front of fires while the wind howled and blew thick, grey mists about. Rain and sleet washed over the land, stabbing like knives, turning the roads into sucking mud morasses between washed-out bridges and icicle-hung trees. Grey clouds chased each other across the sky, trapping the smoke of hearth fires and turning the air malodorous and stinging. People walked with scarfs over their mouths, coughing when they inhaled.

Isabel, Duchess of Clarence, didn't go out. She watched her husband pace like a bear on hot coals and wished he'd notice her newly lotioned skin, the colour once more brightening her cheeks.

"George, let's dine alone tonight. It's foul outside. I'm weary of Westminster. Everything there is drab."

"If I were King, it would be festive." His pacing increased. His velvets and furs were regal purple and ermine. His hair golden as a crown. "What am I, Isabel? Your father's loyal appendage? Nothing. It was not so when we first planned."

She lifted a glass of warmed wassail. Their private solar

smelled of evergreens and spicy Christmas herbs. The servant Ankarette had seen to that. "George, my father is sore beset. He can't turn England around overnight. Even for Warwick the people are afraid to cheer as they once did. Times are so strange."

George too drank wassail. He'd been drinking all day. His speech slurred. "Isabel, my love, don't you see? I'm like a man in the boot. Only it's my whole self and not just a foot being crushed. You've never seen it. Blood and flesh ooze out. Bones crack. So it is with my hopes. Warwick has nothing to offer." His mind reverted back to its overriding theme. "Your father promised me a crown."

"He must be careful, George. When the rest of the Lancastrians get here, he can act more forcibly. He knows Edward plots and schemes in Burges, possibly with Duke Charles.

"My father wants to govern well and with temperance." Isabel strained to care. After months of pain and lethargy, she felt wonderful. Her monthly courses had resumed. Her skin glowed. She thanked Ankarette daily for the hours of care. All her women noticed. She patted the pillows beside her. "What can you do, George? Come, give me a little of yourself. Who knows how things will fall out. A crown can roll many ways in a battle."

"I'll never be King." The wine and liquor overcame the young duke. He sat down sobbing. "Isabel, I wanted it for you, too."

She folded him in her arms, wishing he wouldn't drink so much. She knew he had received secret missives from his sister in Burgundy. She had to hold him to her father's side. And her side. She kissed his forehead. "George, I can bear children again. Don't think of politics for a few hours." She sensed his remoteness. "We'll have an astrologer cast a horoscope. I wager he'll see you as King." She tried to think of a royal brother who had become King and could remember only John, of evil reputation, who had signed the Magna Carta. She caressed his back. "George, the Prince of Lancaster is only one man. He has never fought in battle." She stopped horrified at what she said. She spoke of Anne's husband. Her thoughts drifted briefly to her sister. She wondered how little Anne found married life. George fell asleep against her shoulder, his mouth hanging open, his breath heavy with drink.

Above the palace of Des Trounelles in Paris, the dark sky of winter was powdered with gold, blue and red lights shot forth with a roar of powder. Louis flaunted another of his special enthusiasms, fireworks. Watching from the window, Anne thought each burst more beautiful than the last. It must have been the King and royal family had arrived at Des Trounelles; every citizen within the old walls of Paris would surely see such a display and know its significance. Reluctantly, she left the window and returned to a glowing brazier, trying to warm herself.

"*Est-ce que vous avez froid, Madame?*" The serving-maid, who had been smoothing the bed-sheets, wrinkled her forehead in concern. "It would be possible to have another brazier, some hot broth?"

"I've eaten." She tried to stop shivering. "I became chilled on the road. It's a long journey." Anne studied her hands. How blue the veins were! They had already been in Paris three nights, yet she was still cold and weary. She recalled vividly the five plodding days of travel. The icy wind had torn at them. It moaned a dirge, the hoofbeats of the horses were a dull, persistent counterpoint. Several of the group had fallen sick, their bowels loosened by course journey food. They had crouched, groaning behind bushes, while the stinking brown fluid stained the snow. The first day the jolts of the road streaked through her groin, into her stomach. By evening she could hardly move. Yet the malaise, which had come on the final day, a sore throat and a little fever, had not diminished inside the thick walls of the royal residence. She could not define her illness except in terms of exhaustion which left strength for nothing but indifference. Let Edward demand as he would, let the road be endless and the winds forever. What did it matter now? Indifference had become her escape.

"Madame should watch the fireworks." The serving-girl gestured toward the window. "They're especially fine. We've had such shows in Paris since before I was born. It's especially nice when they shoot lights over the Seine and the river reflects. They do that when a criminal and ape are sewn in a bag together and drowned."

Anne nodded. "Is Olivier, the barber-surgeon, with the King?" She was surprised at her own question. Surprised too at the rasping hoarseness in her voice.

"*Mais oui*. Olivier is always with the King."

"A good night then." Anne closed her eyes, too tired to even get ready for bed. Perhaps Edward wouldn't come. She knew his mother objected with increasing shrillness. She had to see Olivier who knew about cures. Tomorrow. Perhaps she'd feel better. She wondered if it was Christmas tomorrow or were there still some days to go? Time had blurred and become a wilderness of distortion. How hot the brazier burned! She felt giddy, feverish. She couldn't find air enough to breathe. A new pain burst in her right side, twisted through her. She had to get to bed. Anne stood up, swaying, dragged herself, her feet all entangled in her gown, across the room. The pain made her gasp and she pressed her hand hard against her side. Carefully, inching along, she reached the bed and fell across it.

She dreamed someone undressed her with great

gentleness and wrapped her in covers. It was Dame Elinore, her face white as snow, who propped her on pillows while Olivier, a tiny, dancing dwarf, plied warming-pans and filled the air with spicy scents. Somewhere at the very edge of her dream, Edward paced about; but her mother sat close. Unknown faces peeked from the folds of the bed-curtains. A knife wrote bloody messages she couldn't read. An infant hand pressed coldly against her lips. Words floated on the air as from behind muffled furs. "She coughs blood," someone said and Anne wondered of whom they spoke. "Her nails are blue. She must have more air." Perhaps that was Olivier's heavy voice. Anne didn't understand. "My side. My side!" She whispered and screamed it, over and over. Could no one hear her?

"Is she dying?" The Prince found sickness repulsive. Medicine stank. The sick always puked. He thought his wife looked wizened, her hair dull. Still he didn't want her to die. Her passive acceptance of his demands made him feel masterful, a man of the world instructing a child.

"She is very sick." Olivier stared up at the Prince. The humpback hated all straight-legged tall men. He knew a little trick with a tiny knife, a mere snip behind the knees, and the Prince would never stand tall again. "Above all she must have total rest."

The countess looked from the deformed doctor to the Prince and placed her trust in the misshapen man. She felt overwhelmed by grief. Somehow she'd let this happen to Anne. Her beautiful daughter had never been sick before, even in the terrible cold of Yorkshire. She'd been blind not to see how thin the girl was. Blind because she couldn't bear to see. And now Anne might die.

For Anne all traces of reality faded. She was alone in a dark world slashed by green lights. Distorted shapes twisted into red coils and became ragged staffs. Fields of green spread out and receded. Castle walls rose and crumbled. Invisible horses whinnied. Flowers bloomed, gigantic, brilliant, only to explode and bloom again. Purple, they were always purple. Thistles. She knew them. It was their spikes which stabbed her side. And then blood dripped, immense drops, rain, tears, blood, all fell together. She heard weeping. A night of weeping. The lights vanished. The last flower exploded. The blood changed from red to black. Everything was black. In the blackness shadows reached out to her, grotesque, not quite seen, forms that tore at her throat and pierced her side. She screamed and they screamed back. She pleaded to escape the dark and the images mocked her. She was very tired, too tired to even cry out or protest when the shadows blended into one long, dark tunnel at the end of which there was light. She struggled toward the light. It had to mark the end of suffering. She couldn't breathe. Her legs had no strength. She would crawl. Eternity waited. The last shadow flickered on the walls of the tunnel and faded. The light, it must have been death, was nearer.

"Pray for us sinners now and in the hour of our death," someone murmured.

"It is not the hour of her death." Her mother's voice.

Dimly she saw the light was only a priest dressed in white. He held a golden crucifix.

"Make a good act of contrition, my daughter," he said.

Anne reached toward the cross. If she touched it, even with her mind, there would be nothing but light. Of this she was sure. Light and nothing else. Nothing. She drew back and turned her head. Her mother was close. The sacred elements of the Viaticum were laid beside her. Olivier was there, too, his face wet with sweat.

"Hold her up, Madame," he commanded the countess. "This is the crisis."

The crucifix was still very close. Anne took a deep breath. "Mama."

Her mother held her with fierce protectiveness. Anne could feel the strength of maternal love. Olivier, his small eyes narrowed in concentration, his hump thrust up, bent over the girl. "It's passing. *Une brave jeune fille.* She fights to live."

Anne leaned against her mother. "Mama, I'm hungry."

Instantly there was activity, a scurrying about, a collective relief. The priest made the sign of the cross over the girl. "God is good," he said. "His mercy endures forever."

Later the countess told her. It had been ten days. Anne Beauchamp had slept on a cot beside her daughter's bed though warned the ill humours of the disease might be contagious. Olivier had sat in the corner by the hour. Perched on a little stool, all humped, he had explained: the air-sacs each person carried in their chests were in Anne filling with liquid. For some reason this caused the heart to beat harder. The countess shuddered slightly. Such knowledge could only be gained by the dissection of the dead, a practice forbidden by church and common decency. "He also oversaw your food. Rich soups. Whenever you were not coughing or sleeping, you were fed. Do you remember?"

"I remember the pain in my side."

"Olivier tried hot plasters, but they didn't work. Binding it seemed to give you some relief. The last three days we despaired. You didn't cry out any longer. Olivier was distraught. He forbade the chamber to all but me and the serving-women. I don't understand why he took such care."

"It would be awkward, if I'd died, Mama."

"It was more than that." Her mother frowned in puzzlement then bent and kissed her. "And I tried to give you of my strength, Anne. And love. Could you sense that?" The countess watched her daughter's face. The answer meant redemption or damnation, so deeply had guilt engulfed her.

"Yes." Anne remembered the moment of choice. It had been very real, light or life. "Yes, Mama. You were there."

The countess sighed. A sweet relief she could never explain filled her. "King Louis sent word he was having prayers said for your special intention in all the churches of Paris. Charlotte inquired daily. Edward came by once."

IX

Three weeks later Edward surveyed his wife propped up in bed and listening to her mother read. The countess was in the midst of Chaucer's whimsey of "Chanticleer and Pertelote" which had been secured for them in English. Anne had laughed over it many times in the past. Now Edward brought silence.

"*Nom de dieu*, Anne, you look little. Are you so thin?"

"Not near as thin as I was." She thought of the constant stream of savoury foods prepared especially for her. "I eat all the time."

He glanced about the room. "A mousehole chamber."

"But easy to keep warm."

"I suppose so." He barely suppressed a yawn. "Well then, you will soon be fit. We're impatient to go to England."

"I, too, want to be in England." Anne thought she had never uttered truer words.

"Warwick writes we should come with all possible speed. Your uncle, the one called the Bastard of Fauconberg, has established a sort of control over Channel waters with the aid of King Louis. It's time. Each day matters."

"I'm getting well as fast as I can. When you're ready, I'll

be." Edward, she noticed, had thrived in Paris. His cheeks were ruddy, his body a bit thicker. Paris was said to be a lively city.

"We'll go to Honfleur and then to England. The French hold Amiens. Duke Charles, for all his Burgundian pride and temper, won't bother us. I think Louis hates the duke because Charles has fine legs." Edward grinned. "And by St Jude, Louis's legs are curved as bowstrings."

"A great asset on horseback," the countess said quietly. "Edward, there's no point in further talk which only tires Anne. My daughter will travel as soon as she can. No one wants to get to England more than we two."

"Sentiment." Edward let the yawn escape. "Well, Madame, none of us wait patiently." He strode to the door. "Get well soon, wife."

Anne watched him leave. The gulf of her sickness stretched between them. He was on the other side talking politics, planning battles. She felt cleansed by the fever's fire. Her body healed. She did not care to find a crossing-place to be with Edward. She turned to her mother. "Read me that poem, please. The one King Louis recommended."

"Ah, François Villon's song."

"Yes, the refrain. I like it."

"Villon is a rogue. He's not been heard of since Louis banned him from Paris. He reminds me of Malory."

"Malory?"

"Remember, Anne. A shabby man. He looked older than his years. He served my father, your grandfather, at Calais. He was even a member of Parliament from Warwickshire and the owner of a fine manor. Then he turned to writing, the legends of King Arthur." Her mother's face was briefly youthful with happy memories. "He told those legends to you, at least some of them, when you were a child at Middleham."

"He had a scraggly beard." The scene focused. "It was in the Presence Chamber. The chandelier had new candles. I remember. I sat on pillows with Richard. We stayed up so late. Oh, those were marvellous stories."

"And Malory a marvellous rogue." Anne Beauchamp laughed. "He stole from abbeys, terrified the nuns, even swam a moat after one escapade. Yet he rendered my family good service. I don't know where he is now, even if he lives."

"Richard liked the stories, too."

"I know, Anne." Her mother hastily searched among the pile of papers. "Here is the refrain. It is lovely. And strangely sad.

" 'Nay, never ask this week, fair lord,
Where they are gone, nor yet this year,
Save this much for an overword –
But where are the snows of yesteryear?

Mother of God, where be they then –
But where are the snows of yesteryear?' "

Anne thought of Richard sitting beside her at Middleham, as they listened to Malory's tale. In the leaded window of the Presence Chamber the family emblem blazed in stained glass. A new table with an inlaid chessboard was the main piece of furniture along with some joint-stools and one chair. Cushions, bright as jewels, were scattered about on the floor. And Richard ate an orange. He peeled it and they shared segments. She wouldn't think of it. Where indeed were the snows of yesteryear?

In Burgundy the snow was pure, a smooth crystaline blanket. Icicles sparkled. The palace of Duke Charles sparkled. Tile floors, scrubbed daily, gleamed; tapestries, freshly brushed, kept in warmth; and all the fireplaces were walled and had chimneys.

Charles of Burgundy, dressed in enough jewels and furs to outfit several fleets, faced his brother-in-law Edward of England who wore borrowed clothes and rented gems. Edward's cap was on his head but should have been in his hand. He came to beg.

"A great amount." Charles glanced at his adviser Phillippe de Commynes. Did de Commynes think it too much? France had declared war on Burgundy. Duke Charles had new black armour rich with niello work. He'd left the rest of any preparations to de Commynes. War with France was tedious. Not at all appropriate for the season.

Edward smiled. "A small amount to you, Charles. Come, you are the wealthiest man in Europe." Edward thought Charles proud as a peacock and peacock-brained. Vanity was the route of appeal.

"Fifty thousand crowns." Charles took a half minute to say the words. "Have you talked to my wife?"

Richard, standing beside his brother, bowed and nodded. "At Lille. She's in touch with George of Clarence. She will write again. She has such sweet memories of little George when we all were young at Fotheringhay."

Charles spared Richard one glance. He was short, dull. Of course, de Commynes was dull, too. But brilliant. Charles sent a desperate mental message to his adviser who had withdrawn to a far corner.

Phillippe de Commynes had been wondering if he served the wrong master. Louis of France made all the right moves. Charles, unless carefully watched, all the wrong ones. Life was a chess game. He had every intention of being on the winning side. Still, he was a Burgundian.

He smiled cynically at Edward. "Do you propose, your

grace, to use the old trick, I believe it dates from Henry of Bolingbroke, later Henry IV, that you return to England but to claim your estates? A hazardous venture at best."

Edward answered the smile, putting all his charm and bright intellect into his words. "I've heard you're a master-politician who guesses thoughts. So I plan. It will work. We can sail by March. England will greet me with open arms. London will have garlands in the streets. I know my country." He turned to Charles. "France and her spider King will skulk home. You'll have time for the hunt, for jousting."

Charles shuffled uneasily. "If I can afford it." He gazed at Richard. The boy was small, lacking all importance, yet de Commynes had told him to take heed of Richard of Gloucester.

"What's in this for you?" His huge hands slapped together. "Got a doxy waiting in England?"

"I fight with my brother." Richard couldn't muster warmth and affinity for this brother-in-law. He thought of Warwick. They all fought for survival and none knew it more than Warwick. It would be a bitter contest between men who had respected, and loved, each other. Even Edward, the greatest warrior of the age, didn't rejoice in the coming battle. It was simply a matter of necessity. He glanced at Edward. His brother looked tense. The humility of a supplicant was hard to maintain.

"And the new little Prince born in sanctuary?" De Commynes slid into the silence. "He will give you a royal welcome."

"As will my Queen." Edward sounded convincing. He thought of the Queen with mild interest. She would have her demands ready. She always did and, in the night when her soft curved hips met his, he always gave her whatever she asked.

The Woodvilles. Richard pictured a dung-heap filled

with maggots – no, the Queen's kin were far more deadly: a canker sore at the heart of England, ripe with yellow pus and stinking corruption. Ever since Edward had married Elizabeth Woodville her family had advanced. Her five nubile sisters were married to wealth and ranks, her five brothers equally flourished. And none was in sight when needed. Anthony Woodville was the only one in exile with them. The rest of the curs had found safe kennels. But they'd return to Westminster when Edward did. Ready for more bounty and no responsibility. He knew they had nothing but contempt for him. He wasn't one of the handsome, witty ones. He should be gay, convivial and above all unfettered by morals. Richard wondered he could love Edward when his brother let this tribe of sycophants flourish even while his years of Warwick's friendship were lost in neglect.

He pulled himself back to the present and saw de Commynes watching him. The man's eyes were hawklike. "I can sway the North for my brother." He said it without boasting for the North was the home of his heart.

Duke Charles yawned. "De Commynes, do I have fifty thousand crowns to spare?" He remembered he'd beaten his chief adviser in chess the hour before. He didn't think de Commynes had let him, at least not this time. He'd give the man back his self-respect.

"You do, your grace. And well spent. France will stop warring when York returns to England." Better to spend it for fighting in England than for the unstable defences of Burgundy. Charles looked splendid in his armour and was totally irresponsible.

Charles waved his jeweled hands. "So, then, it's yours, brother-in-law. And we'll make Louis very angry."

Edward slapped Charles on the back. "We are unbeatable. I know it."

At Vespers Edward and Richard gave thanks in the gleaming chapel of Charles's palace. The smell of incense closed about them. The priest glowed in his green chasuble, the season's holy colour.

Below the chanting Richard asked, "Have your agents in Paris heard ought of Anne?"

"She's married." Edward glanced sideways at his brother. "She was sick, but Louis had masses said for her. She's better. So I heard today."

"You didn't tell me."

"Why add to your anguish? You could do nothing. Her mother is with her."

"I'll kill the Lancastrian with my own sword. I swear it."

"No. The sickness was a lung fever. Not a fault of the marriage-bed, Dick. Let someone else kill him. Then, if perhaps the girl has grown fond of her husband, she won't blame you. She'll probably got to a nunnery."

The wisdom of the advice was unarguable, yet Richard shook his head. He didn't particularly want to kill the Prince, who was even younger than he. He just wanted Anne – free. Free of marriage, free to love him. He wondered miserably if love could survive all that had happened. Would happen. The priest chanted on. The incense hovered in great clouds. Richard prayed his familiar prayer. Anne. God and the Blessed Mother guard her.

On March 11, Charles of Burgundy, his stomach hollow with nausea and the loss of fifty-thousand crowns, petitioned St George. "Let them win."

The Yorkists sailed in spite of heavy seas.

X

King Louis believed in taking all possible precaution. Though the pin jabbed his fingers, he stuck a medal of St George in his cap. He'd take St George out as soon as England was safely won. His cap already sagged with medals.

For each of the departing English, Louis had ordered St Christophers. These, too, were lead. He handed them out as they waited, huddled in the cobblestoned courtyard. He talked rapidly as always. "May the fog clear. The crossing be quick and easy. You will see the alliance with France is ratified."

He took hold of Margaret's arm. "*Chère cousine*, my citizens pay taxes on hearth, wine and salt to support your Enterprise of England."

Margaret's eyes were as hooded as the King's. She didn't answer.

Louis pressed her hand. "Godspeed. When you're in England you'll remember all I've done."

Margaret shrugged. "I'll follow my own counsel."

Louis shuddered. Her own counsel had led from mishap to disaster. Women were fools.

He turned to the countess and Anne. "I understand Sir

John Wenlock has joined your cause. Didn't he refuse you at Calais?''

"Wenlock is a friend." Anne Beauchamp was quietly happy. "He kept us from being trapped at Calais. Once in the harbour the Yorkist fleet would have encircled us. A true friend."

Louis bent over their hands. "So then. All omens are good. A mild day in February. Even the sky is blue. That is for you, Lady Anne. Remember me to your lord father when you're once again in England."

Charlotte, her round face both happy and anxious, handed Anne a small, perfumed ball. "Ships smell, well, like the ocean and rotting timbers, or so I'm told. So you must have flowers to remind you the voyage will soon be over. God willing."

Slowly, with amazement, Anne recognized the stirring of hope. No longer did the days stretch in endless emptiness. All the uncertainties of tomorrow were submerged in the knowledge the way now pointed to England. Anne climbed into a horse-supported sedan-chair. "*Au revoir*, your graces. *Merci. Merci beaucoup.*" She'd never see any of them again. She was going home.

Pennants and banners were raised. Trumpets called. The accompanying soldiers began to file out. Margaret gave shrill orders to her retinue. A cannon fired to hail their departure.

Riding in comfort, Anne could imagine it was spring. The pillows in the chair were scented with dried flower-petals, warming-pans nestled at her feet. She thought of Olivier. Such conern was surely his parting gift.

They delayed at Honfluer, for Margaret would not put out to sea to be buffeted by violent winds.

It was not until April Uncle Fauconberg and a season of mild weather finally coaxed Margaret to leave Honfleur.

There'd been no certain news for a month. Wenlock had heard the rumour Edward of York and his men were back in England but knew no more. Anne stood on the deck as the Lancastrian ships slipped out of the harbour and thought of that tall Plantagenet King who, for all his faults, was much loved. He called the citizens of London by name, traded along with the merchants for profit, had never known defeat. Her father had his own legend and a great many cannons. Would it be enough? She could talk to no one. Victory, Lancastrian victory, in this place there was nothing else to be said. And she was alone. Her mother's thoughts leaped ahead to reunion with her husband. John Fortescue was on another ship. Margaret of Anjou ignored her. The Prince was busy with battle strategies. Anne treasured her aloneness; in that silent time she found strength.

The crossing was slow. They left the countess at Portsmouth. Wenlock insisted she take shelter in Beaulieu Abbey until they knew the state of things in England.

Her mother's farewell was tearful. She held Anne in her arms and wept as she whispered words of encouragement. "Wenlock will be with you, daughter. There's no need to fear. Your father rules the realm."

The girl brushed aside her tears. "Nor need to weep."

Her mother took the coral rosary from a purse. "Keep this, Anne. It is worn with prayers. It's all I have."

"Oh, I couldn't. It's too precious."

"And so you must have it." Her mother hugged her child closely again. "Courage, always. Like your father."

Anne put the rosary in her own purse still emblazoned with the Warwick emblem. "I love you, Mother. God be with you."

"And with you, Anne. Always."

In the red-hued dusk of mid-April, while the sun touched

the distant horizon and the ocean glistened in the low light, the main group of ships landed at Weymouth on the south coast of Dorset. Orders were given, the gangplank banged down, seamen swore, shouted and gave thanks for a safe crossing. Unnoticed in the noisy confusion, Anne ran down the gangplank laughing at her own excitement. She listened to the calling of English voices, inhaled the noxious stench of fish, seaweed and rotted wood, saw the greenness of the mossy pier and the deep shadows of ale-houses with the projecting poles that marked them thrusting far out above the doors. Bending down, she joyfully scooped up a handful of sand and gravel. It was damp and cold and dirty, but she held it, pressing the mixture into a ball, a small portion of England.

"Princess, we're to go to Cerne Abbey for the night. Queen Margaret has arranged it. They're kind to wayfarers."

Anne smiled at Wenlock. "We're hardly wayfarers. Couldn't we ride toward London? Why is no one here to meet us? What is going on? Isn't today Easter?"

Wenlock nodded. "So what should we fear on a holy day? The saints are with us."

Richard Neville, Earl of Warwick, was beyond fear. Margaret was said to be on her way. She came too late, far too late. In a few hours fate would demand resolution, for Edward of York had returned to England and the realm had rallied to him. At Coventry, Edward had challenged him while he had stood on the city walls and looked out and seen all he had created: The man he'd made King, a giant in armour, and Richard of Gloucester, a slight, proud figure beside him. The black bull symbol of Clarence had been in the foreranks, too. He'd not been surprised. Clarence was born to play false.

In an agony of self-knowledge, Warwick had realized he could not fire on those men. He felt as though his heart were dead. Did anyone think how close he'd come to almost fulfilling the great design he had created. He had bound men together by sheer force of his personality, his bounty, his unquestioned leadership. King in all but name. Almost. The word of failure. When time ceased.

Bitterly he had learned only moments before that for Louis of France time's wheel spun with fresh, remorseless vigour. Obviously hearing of Edward's return, Louis had made peace with Burgundy and thus with a Yorkist King, if Edward won. Bile soured his mouth. For the few months allowed him, Warwick had staked his rule on Louis' loyalty.

Tonight on the field of Barnet the day's red ending might be the last sunset he'd ever see. No longer could he check the tides of fortune. The royal forces were near. A fog was closing about his camp. He hated the thought of dying in the fog. In anguish and anger he wrote Louis. Black stabs of letters accused the French King of perfidy and treachery. He'd throw away what might have been his last refuge. A final blaze of self if his star fell.

His men were drawn up on a rise of ground about a mile north of Barnet. It was a great plateau, four hundred feet above sea-level. Oxford was there. And John Neville. None was sure of the position of the King's men somewhere in the fog near the village. Warwick ordered his cannons to fire into the darkness. Probably a futile gesture, flinging stones into nothingness.

He walked among his men a while and found them ready. They knew they outnumbered the Yorkists, and they had the good ground. He withdrew to his tent.

"So, Richard, tomorrow will come. I'm glad."

He saw with a start John Neville sat on a joint-stool by

the portable writing-desk. His younger brother had grey in his hair, despair in his eyes.

"John, we can't lose. Not with you at my side."

John Neville looked away. "Edward of York has never lost a battle."

"He's only human." Warwick felt a cold shiver. John wanted to die. He could see his face, drained of all but the need to end the tearing of his soul between King and brother.

"Richard, you were my idol. Yet tomorrow I'll wear two badges. One the Bear and Ragged Staff. The other the Sun in Splendour. I don't know which one will be over my heart."

"John, you'll not betray me. We can win."

"I have no betrayals left." John Neville rose and embraced his brother. "Till we meet again. Beyond the field of Barnet." He paused a moment. "Beyond ambition."

"John, you'd hex us. Would you bring ill fortune down?"

John Neville paused at the tent flap. "Richard, I blame no one. I can't follow this road. I am as I am. What are you, my brother?" He was gone into the night.

Warwick sank down on the pallet. He wished John had stayed. They could have talked of their boyhood in the North. The good years. What was he? He was Warwick the Kingmaker. He stood for himself. For close to six years he had been moving toward this hour, this battle. He would win. Why would God create him with such passions only to destroy him? He slept a little and awoke to knowledge. He had betrayed himself. He had turned his back on all the best. The reasons had seemed sufficient at the time.

The guard told him it was four o'clock. Easter Sunday. The day of final resolving. His squires dressed him. He knew he must take the same risks as the common soldiers in

the coming mêlée or they'd think he meant to desert. He'd
fight on foot. And damn them all. The fog still hung a wet
blanket over both camp and town. The banners were limp.
The trumpets sounded thin. It was time. He thought of his
wife, Isabel, and Anne. For them he had to have the day.
For them. For himself. The legend in which he existed. He
had no battle-cry. He fought for Warwick, for glory, for
survival.

John Neville led the troops. The centres crashed and
locked. Warwick supported his brother with a contingent of
his own household guard. The fog hid the battle in a grey
mist. Swords crashed, horses screamed, men cursed and
died. Warwick brought up men from the rear when the line
weakened. He planned, in an instant, new strategies and
gave strength by the sheer force of will and voice. The Bear
and Ragged Staff banner floated high, a portent of triumph.
"To Warwick," he shouted and the men came. An hour,
two hours passed. Warwick's ranks swayed but did not
give. Edward of England led the men hammering at his
centre. They yelled, swore and failed to advance.

Warwick glimpsed victory. Edward couldn't break his
lines. God. St George. If only the flanks held. He could not
know that in the fog the outer lines of the army had twisted.
Oxford's banner of the Star and Streams had been
mistaken for the Sun in Splendour. In a moment so cold it
froze his heart he heard the shout, "Treason."

Men began to creep, run away. He could hear the clash
as the King led another charge. He struggled to bring up
more reserves. John fought on with a dreadful tenacity.
Oxford's men fled. Panic ripped through the remaining
forces. Dimly in the fog Warwick could see the Sun in
Splendour banner bearing down on his brother

He stood for a moment. He must get a horse. There was
always another day. Arrows whined near him. He looked at

his banner, still tall and untouched. His brother was down. Suddenly he was alone. Triumph was everywhere except where he stood. He heard the shouting. He knew those voices. Instinct made him turn to where the horses were tethered.

He never saw the men who clawed the helmet from his head, tearing his skin. The knife-flash was his last reality. He thought with wonder how bright the blade.

The King and Richard found him as common soldiers stripped his body. The King, covered with mud, hoarse from almost three hours of fighting, bent over the still figure. He had ordered his life spared. Yet it was better this way. Better to die while still alive than decay in the Tower over the years.

Richard, slightly wounded in the side, mourning the death of his favourite squire, joined his brother and together they looked down on the man who had wrought such havoc.

"I could never imagine him so. Bloody. Old." Richard moved stiffly. They had won. He'd never known such sadness.

Edward put his arm around him. "Warwick," he said slowly, "burned too brightly. He was consumed."

Edward rode to collect his forces and congratulate his lieutenants.

Richard stood staring down at the mangled face, the skin stripped from the nose, tangled grey hair and shredded flesh where the armour had been torn away. So life ended. Heaven was a blank. Yet Warwick had lived, thought Richard, he lived to the utmost. Perhaps he'd welcomed the knife.

XI

Two days later Edmund Beaufort, Duke of Somerset, whose father had died fighting for Lancaster, appeared at Weymouth. His face was haggard, his arm stiff with a wound. Gulping wine, he ignored the proffered food. "Barnet, a Hell. Stinking of Hell," he mumbled and looked at no one. "Gunpowder. A cursed fog."

Margaret and Edward listened in fury. Anne felt the scene with an unmitigated vividness that took her far from the snug, comfortable parlour of the abbey and the distant chanting of Matins. Outside the leaded windows the sun shone, but clearer to her was the fog of Barnet. Somerset tried to explain the confusion, the distrust.

"I've seen battle. I know men run." Margaret began a rhythmic pacing up and down the room. "And so?"

Somerset slumped, his eyes on the floor. "Warwick is dead, Madame. Also his brother, John Neville." He paused.

"Warwick!" Fear raced with joy through Margaret's mind.

"They stabbed him, many times. In the neck. So it's said." Somerset put his hands over his face and closed his eyes.

Even as they arrived in England. Anne let the tears run

down her face. She would never see him again. He had sold his honour, and finally his life, in pursuit of his own dream of himself. She felt no bitterness because he had also sold her. Now he was dead she could love him fully again. Dead. No bells would toll for him. No masses said. Anne put her hands over her face. It was over for him. Rest in peace. Oh, rest in peace, Father. She became aware that Wenlock watched her anxiously. He, too, grieved. Anne was glad he forbore hollow words of comfort.

"If I had been there, we'd have won."

Somerset answered the Prince tonelessly. "Your grace's presence might have made some difference."

"The difference between victory and defeat. Warwick was an old warhorse, ready to be mowed down."

Anne stood, loathing Edward. "He was a man, husband, such as you can't even comprehend." She left them all. Only she grieved. On the face of Margaret fear was giving way to joy. An enemy was dead.

By supper, decisions were made. The Duke of Somerset, revived by food and rest, spoke of what had to be done. Anne half listened. The evening was warm for April; there was a bouquet of early daffodils on the table, yellow as the sun. She'd wept that day, but now she felt remote. What further did she have to do with these people or their feverish planning? With her father dead, she was a nonentity and would be treated so.

All designs were completed. The Countess of Warwick should stay in sanctuary. Anne would accompany the Lancastrian train; thus keep whatever remained of Neville support.

"The Earl of Devon and many loyal men will flock to the Lancastrian banner. Your graces will be stars to follow," Somerset predicted. "Also, recall the Welshman, Jasper Tudor. He commands a friendly and fierce army in Wales.

He's eager to join the Lancastrian cause. Barnet doesn't mean the end of Lancaster. Richard of Gloucester has been slightly wounded and his squire killed. The time's ripe for Lancaster as never before.'' The duke's confidence was total.

Margaret of Anjou bit dry lips. "Edward of York is mighty in battle. A bloody monster.'' She looked at her son. "I don't know if fate smiles on us. I'm plagued with doubts. Fear gnaws at my heart.''

"By my faith.'' Sir John Fortescue, who had sat quietly through the early discussion, leaned forward. "Madame, as a friend through these long years, may I state it plainly? To go back to France is obscurity for the Prince here. The only other choice is to fight this Yorkist foe. Edward of York is but a hulk, a large target. Richard is a runt. You'll never have another chance. You must see that.''

Margaret hunched her shoulders forward in indecision. "I'll never have another chance if my son is dead.'' She could barely say the words.

John Morton, Bishop of Ely, who'd joined them in France, crossed himself. "Surely God will not allow such disaster, Madame. I think if we can join the Welsh, they're zealous fighters, all will be well.''

"You have striven long and hard, Mother.'' Edward regarded her uneasily. "Now let me carry on the fight. Somerset says men will flock to our banner. We mustn't let the prize slip by. And it will be all ours. No grasping Warwick need share in the glory.''

No one even glanced at Anne.

Somerset was reborn that evening. "Recruits can be raised in the West Country. When we join the Welsh, we'll be invincible.''

"Must my son fight in the battle to come?'' Margaret didn't seem to listen.

"Of course I must." Edward went red with annoyance. "Would you have me called a coward?" His mother's protectiveness bit into his vitals. God, she wanted him chaste and craven. He wasn't Prince of a monastery.

"He will be our inspiration, Madame, and we'll keep him safe even in the press of combat."

"I can take care of myself." Edward scowled at the duke. "And shit on the Yorkists."

Anne stood slowly and walked toward the mantel at the end of the dining-hall. Scraping his bench forward Sir John Fortescue let her pass through Margaret's words, "What value is she now?" grated on the air.

Turning at the hearth, the girl looked at them. The oak board from which they had eaten had been cleared and she noticed how white her hands were against the dark wood. She saw John Fortescue smile, but she couldn't return his gentle salute.

"Well, wife?" Edward cocked his head. "You have something to say? Not that it matters."

Anne looked from one to the other. Indeed, how could she convince them of anything? Wenlock might have done so, but he'd ridden that evening to take the tidings to her mother. "I know the Yorkists," she began.

"Aye, we know of Neville love for York," Margaret laughed. "You can watch them die."

Anne ignored her. "You don't speak of George, Duke of Clarence. I'm sure he fights with his brothers. So the three brothers are together. I know them. They can't be beaten."

Edward laughed. "Anne, you're a fool. Anyone can be beaten."

"Possibly even you."

Startled, then angered, Edward cursed her. "You talk like a damned witch." Maybe the chit mourned her father. "You need a priest, wife."

Anne ignored him. "I'll not delay you. You see the possibilities or you don't. We may not reach Wales. It's a long march. The Yorkists move quickly." Anne paused, her thoughts confused. "I've spoken the truth, believe what you will. I don't care."

Edward grabbed her arm. "By God, Anne. You'd put a curse on us. Get out."

His grasp made her arm tighten with pain. "Edward, you're my husband. I don't want to live with the knowledge I sent you to your death."

He pushed his wife from the room and she left in silence. In the tiny chamber allotted to her, solitude brought no sleep. People, memories, questions possessed her mind. What did Isabel think of George's defection? Her father and uncle were dead many hours now. Had either dreamed of such a moment when all alternatives sunk to one? Uncle John might have hoped to die. They'd be given honourable burial. The Yorkists didn't desecrate the dead. How her mother must have been grieving! Where would she be when all was over? An exile again? It was the second night in England; already the whirlwind raged. At the centre was death. Anne moved restlessly about on the narrow cot; at least what ever was to be would be in England.

The Lancastrian train moved slowly north from Cerne Abbey across the swelling land of Dorset Heights to Somersetshire, the Polden Hills and the Brue river valley. Small detachments were sent in the direction of London, pretending to be advance scouts, in the hope Yorkist spies would assume the whole army marched toward London and King Edward would prepare the capital for war. In reality Margaret urged her forces to press for Wales.

"We must unite with the Tudors," she shrilled. Her voice grew hoarse. "Look at the men who come to our banners.

Untrained. They want booty. They've no horses." She glared at her captains, Somerset and Devon. "A bunch of thieves for an army. I know about Wells. The episcopal palace was plundered by my men. Am I the only one who heard?"

"Madame, it's hard to live off the land in early spring. The roads are furrowed." Devon thought Margaret neared hysteria. "Several supply-wagons overturned. But we'll get supplies at Bath."

Bath gave them some food and staples. At Bristol Margaret went to the city mayor and council. "Gentlemen, Christian gentlemen." Her voice had become a rasping whisper. "We need food. I'll remember your kindness when I'm at Westminster." She saw their blank faces. "Some money and artillery? We're desperate. A Prince of England, grandson of Henry V, begs your help. For the love of God." They gave her the money and artillery.

Continuing on northward, the army, a long, loosely strung line of semi-armed men, struggled the thirty-four miles to Gloucester. The commander of that city and castle, Lord Richard Beauchamp, slammed the gates. Margaret had no time to negotiate. Scouts informed her that King Edward, at the head of a sturdy army, sped across England in forced marches and hoped to engage the Lancastrians in immediate battle.

Sitting exhausted on her horse, Anne heard the messenger, coughing with dust and alarm, explain in excited amazement. "Edward of York left London and foully denounced your grace as proscribed at Abingdon." Margaret listened, not an eyelid blinked. The Prince kept hitting a tree with his riding-whip, its snap interspersing the hurried words.

"With his brothers he marches across the country. He sent the order to close the gates of Gloucester. Edward of

York wishes to engage us in combat 'fore we can unite with the Welsh," the messenger finished in a rush.

Somerset gloomily eyed the slovenly bank of ill-equipped malcontents and peasants who called themselves an army and who stood listening with all too keen ears. He thought of his kinsman who had died for Lancaster.

"We must cross the Severn River, if not here, then at Tewkesbury." Margaret's voice was strained with fatigue. "I'll not risk battle in this state. You can see the army's not fit." Her hands clenched, the nails cutting. Her body ached with weariness and dread.

"The Yorkists must be tired, too." Prince Edward rode the best horse in the whole army. He alone was exhilarated. "These renegades at Gloucester will be sorry they turned us away."

Anne looked from one to the other in silence. During the whole journey she'd been treated as though she didn't exist. The girl rode alone, alone in sorrow and alone in hope. To make a pretense now that she cared for Lancaster would have been impossible. She tried often not to think at all, but let the warm spring sun, which had come with May, take away the chill of France and the days she longed to obscure in hazy forgetfulness. Yet past became present when Edward was near. Amboise ached in her memory. Always he was part of her uneasy dreams in which his face merged with that of her father's. Yet he was real enough; Anne could see him breathing, hear his muttered curses. It was her father who was forever dead. It was to her father she had pledged this marriage. And now, Anne could hardly think on it, she might spend her life exiled in France with Edward, without country, without love. Surely that too was death.

Waiting for the decision in which she had no part, Anne turned from the grey walls of Gloucester and viewed the countryside. In the fields sheep grazed; there was the tinkle of a bell-wether as the largest of the animals lumbered through the green, spring grass. Wild flowers, yellow celandine, violets and the vivid blue speedwells, bloomed in bright patches along with many daisies. In the far distance she could see workers who shaded their eyes to look toward the city. They watched them as a funeral procession, as the shades of the House of Lancaster. How strange, she thought wearily, she should be here!

From Gloucester, exhausted and unfed, they dragged on to Tewkesbury, forty-four miles in continuous march from the respite at Bristol. The weather continued unseasonably hot; the road became even more rocky and dangerous. Carts could hardly move because of the deep ditches and many hedges. At five in the afternoon the massive Norman Tower of Tewkesbury Abbey became plainly visible, casting a long shadow in the sundown. The army refused to go further. Even the Duke of Somerset, his mercurial personality shifting possibilities, agreed they should stay where they were, for it was a good position, and take what God would send.

Anne wondered, as she had at Angers, if God cared ought for the Enterprise of England.

XII

Standing to one side Anne watched the sluggish disorder. The men didn't make camp. They fell upon the ground, lying in the cool evening as though drunk. A few plodded to the high ground known as "The Gastons" with the town behind them. Some crawled to where the Swillbrook ran on one side of the small hill. Others dropped with their horses beside the foaming Avon. They were deaf to commands. Somerset and John Wenlock, who had rejoined them that day, tried to fashion some sort of defence. Men simply shook their heads and didn't move.

As he rode toward her, Anne could see the hopelessness on Wenlock's face. He dismounted, kissed her hands. "Your mother sends loving greeting in spite of her sorrow, Princess. She's safe at Beaulieu." He looked at the field of scattered men, already limp as the dead. "I wish you were with her."

"And you also, Sir John. Not on that battlefield."

"I'm needed." Wenlock looked back at the scraggily scattered army. "Much needed, in your cause."

She put her hand on his sleeve. "Sir John, don't run into battle for me. Tomorrow, when the Yorkists will surely come upon us, is a day of great danger for you. Be not in the forefront."

"Princess, don't worry. We'll win. You will be Queen someday. Remember the Yorkists must charge up those same foul roads we climbed so painfully today. I have it on good authority we outnumber them by about three thousand men."

Anne shook her head and looked beyond Wenlock toward the south. So close. It seemed any moment Yorkist banners might appear on the skyline. "Sir John, what was done with the bodies of my father and uncle?"

"The bodies, lying in wooden coffins, were shown to the people of London – at St Paul's." Wenlock swallowed. "The King, that is Edward of York, must prove them dead, you understand. They were given honourable burial at Bisham Abbey."

"My paternal grandparents lie there too, Sir John." She again gazed southward. "So they sleep. Beyond all this, beyond caring." Anne was silent a moment. "And King Henry of Lancaster?"

"Back in the Tower." Wenlock wiped perspiration and road dust from his forehead. "It's said your father-in-law understands none of what has passed."

The girl nodded. So he too had escaped in his own way. "Where do we spend the night? This night before ..."

"A small house of religion at Gupshill. It will be adequate and, if there is a battle at dawn, runners will easily keep you informed." Wenlock smiled. "And bring you news of victory."

"It should be safe enough," she agreed. "I'm glad it's close." Anne took Wenlock's hand. It was hard and strong, like her father's. "Sir John, be careful tomorrow."

"I recall you as a child, Anne." Wenlock hesitated, went on. "In those days we all trusted one another. In you, Princess, rests all the worth of the Lancastrian cause." He stopped abruptly as Edward rode up. Only for Anne,

Warwick's daughter, would he lift a sword for this proud ass and his demon mother.

The Prince's face was flushed with tan, exertion and excitement. "Wenlock, you're needed with the men." He dismissed Sir John with a wave of his riding-crop. "Come, wife, you'll not sleep in camp tonight. There's a bed and, perhaps, a hot dinner waiting."

"Wenlock told me. At Gupshill. Do we leave now?"

"Aye. I'll escort you. A sorry bit of horseflesh you have there. Couldn't better be found?"

Edward's annoyance increased as Sir John helped Anne mount the drooping nag. "God be with you, dear friend," she said to the knight. Their hands separated.

"He's a crap-heap. I'd think the flies would follow him." Edward watched Wenlock ride away. "First one side then the other. A dying fish could flip no more."

"He's a friend." Anne glanced at Edward. The Prince hadn't come to her since her sickness. She'd never seen him look happier. The ride was but a short distance. At the gate by the low, uneven stone wall which circled the squat house and dusty yard, Anne turned to him.

"Edward, listen to me." It was hard to speak above the scratching and cheepings of the chickens roaming in the dirt. A mangy hound watched from the gate. She tried. She had to live with herself. "The Yorkists are fierce fighters. The King, who bears the same name as you do, he's huge, a battering ram in battle. Richard of Gloucester will never retreat. He'll die for his brother. George of Clarence is ripe with hate and treachery. They lead a disciplined army. They understand battle."

He grinned down at her, tall on his horse. "A queen-to-be should have a fighting stomach." He dismounted and lifted her down. "Think of an apple, Anne, filled with worms, rotten and brown at the core. Easy to split. So is

York. Tomorrow we'll split skulls and brains will spatter. By midday you can visit a bloody meadow." A new idea edged into his mind. "Do you fear for your cousins, Anne?"

Her throat was dry. "I don't know. Tomorrow is a day of dying."

"For the Yorkists." He nodded in the direction of the dog. "The hounds can eat their guts." He paused, thinking this was not what he'd meant to say. He reached in his leather hip-pouch. On his hand lay a lock of hair tied with a bit of thread. "I'm carrying this into battle. A token of luck."

Anne swallowed. She remembered Amboise. His demands, the humiliation and pain.

Edward put his arm lightly around his wife and kissed her on the forehead. "We'll have to start over again after tomorrow, you and I. In London, where I was meant to be. Soon you'll carry my child in you."

Anne regarded him thoughtfully. He might be right. What did she know of war? He was young, strong, of the blood royal, and that blood raced with battle fever.

"Edward, you long for dawn?"

"Of course. An end of shabby poverty. Battle and glory. Finally."

His face was bright. She closed his hand about the lock of hair. "To glory, then, Edward, to glory."

He pulled her to him. Covered her mouth in a rough kiss. In surprise he realized the child he'd married had become a woman. He wanted her there in the dust and gravel. She was his, but he'd claim her on silken sheets at Westminster.

Anne drew back. "Tomorrow, Edward. Godspeed." She couldn't bear for him to touch her even as her numbed mind admitted a shadow of pity. He wanted so much. He made her think of her father. She knew he watched her.

Turning, she kissed her fingers and raised her hand in salute. For the first time she smiled without fear or enmity at her husband.

Slowly, she walked toward the low, dark doorway. Two monks bowed nervously and made room for her to pass. She heard Edward ride away, saw the bare feet of the monks, smelled the damp decaying rushes of the small parlour and the sharper stench of rancid meat.

God be merciful, she thought miserably. Richard must have been so near. Oh, be careful, my love, her heart pleaded. Tomorrow when the whirlwind pulled them all into the vortex perhaps she'd see him.

Later in the evening Margaret joined her. Anne had been given the same room as her mother-in-law while the Countess of Devonshire and Lady Katherine Vaux were in a smaller, adjacent chamber. Long after the supper of half-spoiled, spiced meat, Margaret knelt at the hard, wooden prie-dieu with her beads falling in clicking rhythm from her fingers. She'd sent her ladies away and ignored Anne. The corded veins in her neck bulged as did those in her hands. Her red-rimmed eyes were tightly closed. She didn't turn from her prayers even when the candle burned low and sputtered out. Watching from among the blankets on a square box-bed, Anne wondered if the woman would stay up the night. Scouts had brought word the Yorkists were closing in. The battle would surely begin in the early morning while the world hovered between night and day.

Anne clasped her own hands in tense anguish. God forgive her, she didn't want Edward to live, her husband, her enemy. If he lived in defeat, she would accompany him back to France where he'd hate her, as symbol of his failure. The faint pity was gone, vanquished by memories of the past year, fear of the future. If he lived in victory, it meant death to Richard. She must have been evil not to pray as Margaret prayed in the darkness. Richard might no longer care for her. So much had happened. How strong was love?

Regularly, Anne turned the hour glass. At midnight she said, "Madame, you should try and sleep. You'll be better able to face what has become today."

Margaret stirred and shifted, seemingly surprised someone else was there. Her face hardened into its accustomed lines. "What care you? You probably pray for the death of my son."

"Madame, I've never prayed for the death of anyone." There was a darkness at the centre of Anne's mind. In truth, she couldn't pray at all.

"How could you, a chit of a girl, know of my love for my son? He's my whole life. It's for him I struggle."

"He knows that, Madame."

"He kissed me and waved good-bye as though he were off to a tournament."

"That is the way he thinks about it, Madame."

"I've seen battle, Warwick's daughter. I know how men die when swords cut them down."

Anne turned away. She'd never seen a man die.

Margaret shifted again upon the prie-dieu and though she gazed at the wooden crucifix above it her words were addressed to the girl. "Go to sleep, if you can. We've nothing to say to each other."

Anne looked once more at the countenance of Margaret of Anjou, attenuated and old as the primal desires that drove her. Tonight there was a new emotion written bleakly across the woman's face – terror. They, two women, wife and mother, should have been able to comfort one another. But the Queen was right. They'd nothing to say.

XIII

In the night Edward of York pushed his footsore soldiers to within three miles of the Lancastrian position. His scouts told him the enemy line was strung out.

"God be thanked." Edward guffawed in joy. "They didn't make it to Wales. We've got them. Taurus rules, Mars is in the seventh house. Ah, they've no chance."

He ordered the wagons, grating and bumping to bring up supplies. His trumpets kept signalling forward. Close. Too close to let the treason-blackened men and bitch Queen escape. He ordered meat and ale for his men.

Richard reported, "The vanguard staggers across the devilish, rutted countryside to take up a position. They'll face Somerset, who commands the right wing."

"I'll see him in Hell," Edward said dryly. He'd tried to befriend Somerset. This was his reward. "And the hedges, Dick? You can get through?"

"With luck." Richard gazed into the night. The Lancastrians made no effort to conceal themselves. They crashed about, lit campfires, yelled curses. "We'll use arrows. Cannons."

Edward nodded. He could almost remember a time when gunpowder was a novelty. Now a cannon could turn a man into flying bits of flesh. Usually only the shoes were left.

He smiled at his brother in the summer darkness. "You're my right arm. Be careful. I'm stationing some spearmen to back you up. Somerset's a strong fighter."

"I'll not break lines." Richard thought of Barnet and the terrible confusion. Tomorrow promised to be a clear, summer day. "They'll take refuge in the abbey, Edward."

"It's not a sanctuary." Edward swore. "Damn each one of them." No man had ever fought so for his crown, his birthright, he was sure, as he did. He'd like to personally roast each Lancastrian. Yet he knew he'd pardon most in the long run. He always did.

"Is Anne nearby?" Richard whispered the question.

"The scouts say she's at Gupshill less than a mile away. With Margaret." He grinned at Richard. "Sing out and she'd hear you."

Richard had no answer. He knew Edward would never harm Anne. Yet so very close. Cannons misfired. Retreating men often cut down all in their paths. He shuddered. Anne, within reach, and he feared for her. No matter what the year had brought, he was sure she was still an innocent.

The dawn of May 4 came early promising bright, clear weather. Dressing, combing her hair, Anne listened for any sound, some indication. They'd all been moving toward this hour. Her father should be here; he was one of the creators of this time. Out there in the morning was the future. They were all meeting at Tewkesbury: betrayal, expediency, ruthlessness, ambition, hate. Could any good come of this? And she? Would she, in some way, be a victim again today? Thirteen months, an endless time, had finally reached its ordained moment.

Abruptly there was the call of trumpets. It could indeed

have been a tournament on a fair May day. Margaret ran quickly to the main door and looked out. Anne pulled her closk about her. The two other women hovered in the background. There was the clear and deadly roar of artillery, twice repeated. Anne's lips moved in words without thought. "Be with us now and in the hour of our death." Richard, she cried in silence, live, live and oh, somehow find me.

The first runner came with news. His face was a wreath of smiles. "Somerset attacked the vanguard led by the young whelp Richard of Gloucester," he told them. "Gloucester and his men floundered. Gave ground. They'll soon be carrion. Bloating in the sun."

Margaret, her face drawn after her night's vigil, nodded and crossed herself. "Good. Now find out about the centre, where my son fights."

Anne said nothing. It was cold in the May morning. Cold at the centre of her being. Richard will fight until he dies for his brother, she'd said it. She felt helpless and clung to the rough door-rim. Close by some glossy blackbirds sang in a pink-blossomed almond-tree. It would soon be warm. All over England, from here to Middleham, people would be busy with routine work, the spring crops, the tending of baby animals, caring very little whether York or Lancaster died upon the field. Anne put her hands over her face, wondering why her cheeks were flushed while her hands were ice. She cared. Oh God, she cared so much!

Richard fighting among the hedges coolly rallied his men. They had to charge Somerset again, he told his captains. Their losses were light. Somerset had shot his arrow. Richard forced himself to concentrate. These men would live or die by his decision. Yet the nearness of Anne was a soft whisper in his mind. He couldn't think of her, not

now, the time to charge. The spearmen signalled their
readiness from the hidden knoll. His heart cried, *Anne*, and
he waved his men on toward Somerset's regrouped lines.
The spearmen howling like imps of Hell crashed down the
hill. Richard's horse whinnied. His trumpeter blared the
advance. Richard was at the front. Always he fought at the
front. *Anne*. The Yorkists soldiers saw the Lancastrian line
waver. They yelled in triumph. Pushed harder. Richard cut
down men whose faces he never saw. His horse jumped
hedges, managed treacherous ditches. He shouted one
command: "Advance." His sword arched in a whirl of light
and dripping blood. He pushed ahead seeing Somerset was
breaking and trying to escape. Damned traitor. The
Yorkists followed. Clamorous, whooping, wheeling their
horses to kill and kill again. Bodies lay all about. Bloody
meadow, he thought, and paused to breathe. *Anne*. She was
near.

At Gupshill Margaret heard the news. Richard of
Gloucester was not beaten. The King's scrawny brother
fought on. It was Somerset who retreated. The messenger
stumbled over the words, fearful of his own report.

Margaret paced about restlessly. Several times she
looked at the horses and then shook her head. The battle
sounds were nearer, more intense.

It was James Gower, Prince Edward's own sword-bearer,
who told them. Wounded and ashen he slid from his horse,
attempted to bow.

"God has forsaken us?" Margaret seized the young man
by the shoulders.

Gower struggled for control. "Madame, the battle goes
so quickly. All is tumult. I was separated from the Prince
when the centre position disintegrated. The Yorkists press
hard."

Anne handed the sword-bearer a cupful of water and he

gulped it. "The Prince fights on. Wenlock's killed."

"Wenlock. No!" Anne's exclamation startled the others. What was Wenlock to them?

"Aye, Somerset killed him. With a battle-axe he crushed his skull.

"Somerset cried treason when he did it, Princess. I don't know more."

Anne sank down on the low, stone doorstep and hid her face as her hair fell about her shoulders. Tight fear grew. Her father, Uncle John, Wenlock, they'd all been at Middleham once – as had Richard. Had fate some terrible cycle to complete? "Fate be kind," she whispered to the hard ground at her feet, knowing it was a plea of futility.

As from a distance Anne heard the voice of the sword-bearer with the pitch of terror mounting in it. "Madame, you and your ladies should take sanctuary. Further from the battle. Now. I'll escort you. We could cross the Avon. There's a boat waiting. A haven in Bushley."

Margaret whirled upon him. "Coward! Craven! Since you leave my son's side, I'll go. Think you I'd leave him to fight alone against those dogs! Oh God, I should never have come to this place of death. I've been betrayed by all. My prayers are unheard. Get me a horse."

James Gower looked about in alarm. "Madame, without armour? Unprotected! It would be futile. You must listen. You can't save your son, but she can." Gower pointed to Anne.

"She! She and her father are the cause of this Hell. Damnation on her."

"She could ride through to the Yorkist front. They'll let her pass. They know Anne of Warwick. She must tell the King and his brothers you agree to *any terms*, a return to France, anything, if they will spare your son. Madame, it's the only chance."

The battle sounds were close, a din pierced by clatter and shrieks. No artillery fired. It must have been almost totally hand-to-hand combat.

Margaret stared at Anne. "Warwick's daughter." Her expression turned from hysteria to one of disbelief. "I should ask a favour of her?"

"It will be dangerous to ride into such a mêlée," whispered the Countess of Devonshire timidly and she crossed herself for no news had come of her husband who commanded the left wing.

Anne stood slowly and faced Margaret. "I can't think of one reason since you cursed and wished me dead at Angers, indeed of one kindness, which would send me on such an errand."

Violently Margaret struck the girl across the face. "Slut. You were always for York. Don't you realize you're nothing, nothing, now that your father is dead? Enough delay. A horse!"

Anne put a hand to her cheek and stepped aside. Let the shrew rush out and die beside her son.

The Countess of Devonshire plucked nervously at Margaret's sleeve. "Madame, the Princess must go. They'll listen, perhaps. At least they'll not kill her. She might save your son."

Gower nodded. "She's the only one, Madame."

Anne sat back down on the doorstep, her face averted. Gower was on his knees before her. "Please, lady, his life is in your hands. Would you have him die?"

The girl looked down at her hands. A life. A young life. There were trumpets close by. He should die, he and his witch-mother.

"Let him save himself."

It was suddenly Margaret who knelt. Her words were disjointed, halting. "My son. All I have. In mercy."

Anne turned away even as she recognized the inner truth. She could not hold a life in her hands and let it slip away. She hated herself, her father, her weakness. She walked toward the spent horse of the sword-bearer. It would have to do. She looked back once. "Margaret of Anjou, you and your son went looking for your Hell."

Before the Queen could reply, Anne was in the saddle, feeling small on the stallion, her hair tumbling down her back. With the reflexes of many years of riding, she turned the horse and cantered out of the gate. Then she urged the animal to a gallop toward the crashing battle.

XIV

Anne didn't look back. Ahead was the vast confusion of the battlefield. Perhaps somewhere in that haze of dust and death she might fall. Yet ahead, too, was Richard and he would smile and be gentle, perhaps. And if she did save Edward there had to be some way here in England to separate her life from his. There had to be or let her indeed die upon the field.

The battle, a surging line of men, moved forward in roaring triumph, carrying the Sun in Splendour banner of York. Morning light touched with golden gentleness the violent scene and, for a moment, Anne couldn't even find the Lancastrian standards. From out of the thick of the mêlée, a group of men suddenly spurred their horses across a field littered with dead, a great meadow of dead, lying twisted on the grass. Other men ran toward the town while some waded into the rivers which had seemed such a safe boundary but were proving death-traps. She urged the tired horse toward the main group of retreating men.

Anne didn't reach them as quickly as the pursuing Yorkists. A banner of blue and gold flashed and fell. She recognized Prince Edward, his horse and shining armour; he spurred toward the abbey. His sword, unbloodied, caught the sunlight as it moved through the air.

Almost upon the group, Anne heard him cry, "Mercy," as he was pulled from his horse. "Mercy." A dozen daggers showed red. The leading Yorkist pulled up his visor and laughed exultantly. It was Clarence. Others came up. A voice asked, as from a great distance, "Who, by all that's holy, is this woman?"

Slowly Anne moved the horse toward the group that surrounded the body of Edward. And she saw him lying there, his sword in his hand and still unstained, his blond hair soft against the grass, for the helmet had been pulled from his head. He was utterly still. There was blood all over his face while his eyes stared up at nothingness. Anne dismounted and walked toward the body. The puzzled men let her pass. She heard George's voice demanding, "Woman, what the Devil?" and didn't look up. So her father had died and she was not there. Anne knelt beside Edward and closed his eyes. Then, turning, she stood, though an inner trembling seized her. Another horseman joined the group and she raised her head, her hair all unbound about her face, the sun in her eyes. "Richard?"

"Anne, oh God." He was off his horse in a moment and by the girl's side. His arm about her waist steadied her. "Come away. You shouldn't see this. Anne, my precious. Thank God you're safe."

"So it's you, sister-in-law, I should've realized." George spoke in high tones of excitement. "Well, I killed your husband. He begged for mercy. I showed him none. Not so fast there, Richard, our brother will want to question her."

Richard's face was streaked with the sweat of battle and his eyes were weary. But he supported Anne as she clung to him. He didn't look at the surrounding soldiers or even Clarence. "Anne, it's as George says. I'll stay with you."

She could see nothing but the face of Richard. All around there was a red haze blurring the terrible convulsed shapes which had been men. The air stank of blood and battle dust. Horses wandered about. Flies buzzed. Trumpets still called. Anne entwined her fingers with Richard's gauntleted hand and waited. His nearness shielded her.

"Anne Neville. This is no place for you." King Edward, tall on horseback, his face flushed with anger and hard as the faces of the dead, stared down at the girl. Though he'd seen Anne but once, he recognized her immediately.

Each word was an individual effort. "I came from Margaret of Anjou. She wanted me to offer any terms for the life of her son. Clarence came first."

The King glanced at the body with those many wounds. "And that's Edward of Lancaster who was also your husband?"

"Yes, your grace. Would you have spared him, if I'd been sooner?"

"He had to die. For the good of the realm." The King's eyes were blue and cold. "I'll give him honourable burial in Tewkesbury Abbey itself, once I clear out the traitors who cringe there trying to use it as a sanctuary though it be none. Where's Margaret?"

"I think by now she and her ladies may have tried to cross the Avon for some hiding-place, perhaps in the parish of Bushley. Please, don't send me back to her, your grace." Anne could barely talk. The King towered above her, life or death his royal right.

"You can't plan to treat her as a prisoner, Edward." Richard, his face set, stared up at his imperious brother. "She was a victim."

"She came riding into battle to save her husband. A loving wife. Isn't that so, Anne of Warwick?"

The King blocked the sun. The world was changing from red to darkness. If Edward of York hated her, it was no wonder. She took a deep breath, fought for control. "There

was never any love. My father forced ..." Edward's long
shadow covered them all. There was a mutter of voices with
George's, a little bored, "I'll send her to Isabel in London.
Let's round up the prisoners. Enough of this." And
Richard's answer, low and determined, "I'll see to her
care." Then an unknown voice urged the King to ride to the
abbey for Somerset himself was hiding there.

Anne listened no longer. All strength had gone and a
weariness, such as she had not known since her illness,
possessed her. She felt herself lifted into a saddle. Her arms
were about Richard; they'd often ridden pillion in
Yorkshire. Anne rested against the hardness of his armour.
It was quiet, just the sound of horses, an occasional
command and the buzzing of insects. Everything was
unreal, dreamlike. She closed her eyes so as not to see the
dead.

"Anne, did you come today looking for me?"

She was too tired for anything but truth. "Richard, it has
always been you."

Richard slowed the horse. Worn. Streaked with dust and
other's blood, he felt only the soft embrace of her slender
arms. He lifted off and his helmet and turned and kissed
her. "Anne, sweeting, I never stopped hoping."

She nestled against him. "I'm afraid I'm dreaming."

"You need never wake, Anne. Dream of delight."

She leaned against Richard. In all the tragic world this
was her reality. She had found him again. His words, the
sound of his voice, the nearness of his body encompassed
her.

"I'll never forsake you, Anne. Rest. All is well." She was
his miracle to cherish forever.

BOOK OF DAYS

PART II – 1471-72

Her and Her Alone

"Sire, I love her and her alone"
Let Morte d' Arthur
Thomas Malory

I

In later years Anne looked back on the days at Tewkesbury as perfect. Lost no longer. Hated no longer. Held in Richard's arms while spring promised summer. And, if they wanted, privacy. She stayed with the family of Stephen Oldenhall who forswore his name by having one of the newest and most comfortable manors in Tewkesbury. He dealt in leather, all its aspects from cow to shoes or saddles. He had a large shop in Tewekesbury, another in Bath, managed by a son, another in Cheltenham. No man in England dyed leather finer, softer, or turned out neater work. Stephen Oldenhall made shoes for royalty. It was to his home Richard brought Anne.

"It's brick." Anne stared at the handsome manor.

Richard took her little hand in his. "Anne, it's comfortable. He has a parlour with a dais and nine bedrooms. A chapel. Windows everywhere. You'll like it."

Joan Oldenhall was waiting at the door. Notified by a squire, she'd spent a busy half hour checking the guest-chamber, the new privy upstairs where the lead pipes led to a cess-pit, the meats and pastries for supper.

She watched, motherly and concerned, as the Duke of Gloucester helped the frail girl from his horse. So this was

Anne of Warwick. Poor wight. She looked like she'd paid a visit to the Devil himself. Anne smiled and Joan saw her lovely face, the shadowed dimples, the finely arched brows. She put her arm around the girl. "We'll take good care of her, your grace. A bath. A hot meal."

Anne turned to Richard. "Don't go. Not yet." Joan Oldenhall smelled of herbs and fresh bakery, but Richard was safety.

He pressed her hand. "Anne, I must be with Edward. We've got to get those traitors out of the abbey." He saw her face go white. Damn it. Let Edward tend to the butchering, he decided. "I'll stay a while with you in the garden."

Joan thought of her own three daughters and laughed. "I'll get ready the bathing-tent. We've sponges, herbs, perfumes. My youngest girl's dresses should almost fit. I'll find a seamstress to take in a few. The garden's to the left, near the well."

By the spring flowers, shading their eyes from the bright glass of Oldenhall's many windows, Anne sat on a bench with Richard. He stroked her hair gently. She was like a crushed blossom, he thought, denied not water but compassion. Yet he knew Anne was strong. He uttered a quick prayer and kissed her gently.

The girl took his hand, turned it, kissed the palm. "Richard, I'll not hold you to a long-ago pledge. We were children."

"But I'll hold you." Richard put her head against his shoulder. "Anne, have you forgotten already. We both came to Tewkesbury. Didn't you sense me near? I knew you were close. God was kind. We found each other."

"So many dead. My father's fault. Margaret's obsession. And her son's." Anne looked up. "Will the King ever pardon me? Will he send me to the Tower?"

"By God's holy angels, no. Do you think I'd stand by and let him anyway? Besides, Edward can't resist a pretty face." Richard was silent a moment. "He'll not add to his guilt. He mourns Warwick in the back of his mind. He was glad when George came over to our side, even though he knows George is fickle as the wind. You never left in your heart, did you, Anne?"

She shook her head. "No. York had my allegiance. Not that it mattered, except to me."

Richard kissed her again and held her tightly. "Sweeting, you've nothing to fear. After you rest, I'll be back. Believe."

"I do, Richard. For the first time in so long." She stood, pushed back her long mussed hair. "When you come again, I'm going to be pretty."

The bath was a revelation. Anne had never seen a bathing-tent before. Above the tub sheeting stretched on a framework. The tub itself was padded with sponges. The soap was scented. Joan Oldenhall and her daughter Harriet tossed the old clothes in a corner until Anne stood naked.

"So much hair." Harriet began to sort out combs. She was a big girl herself with brown curls so tight they fell only a little below her shoulders. "You look like a faery princess, I vow. All white and gold." She smiled happily. Her own young man preferred a bit of plumpness to roll in his hand.

Anne blushed. "I'm too thin."

Joan kicked aside the discarded clothes. "Best burn them. They're probably lousy."

"I had some good clothes." Anne thought back. Her coffer with the dresses made in France had disappeared somewhere in the grinding struggle to reach Wales.

"No matter. The duke'll be buying you silks and velvets." Joan began to wipe Anne with the sponges. The tub water turned grey. Dirt floated to the top. Joan had no mercy. Anne's skin flushed pink with rubbing. The nipples of her breasts puckered and swelled. Joan grinned. "Think you'll wed soon, lass?"

"I don't know." She watched Harriet preparing a bucket of hot herbs and perfumes. "I'll smell good anyway."

Joan whooped. "An' don't think men can't smell. Drives them crazy. Like a stallion among mares."

Harriet bent over the girl. In spite of the sheltering frame of sheeting, she saw Anne's eyes were dark circled. "First you'll sleep. And eat. God's bones, you're thin as a rail."

"I know. I'm hungry." Anne felt dreamy, relaxed beyond measure. She could close her eyes and imagine she drifted on some sun-warmed river, all flower-banked and peaceful.

A great clatter of horses' hoofs raced by the window. She sat up. "Is there trouble?"

Harriet giggled. "Trouble's over. The King's 'bout to execute some traitors. Bet my Walt's there to see."

And Richard, thought Anne. "Did Margaret escape?" she asked without caring.

"So far." Harriet poured the scented water to rinse Anne. "They'll find her. Sir William Stanley, a bristly hog, snorts on the chase."

"He'll tell her about her son?" Anne was glad she wouldn't be there.

"Aye. The old witch will screech. Tear out her hair maybe." Harriet began patting Anne dry. The towel was fluffy. "An' Tewkesbury's the burial place for Edward of Lancaster. People'll come from all 'round. Good for business."

Richard stood to watch the executions. He'd never seen a beheading. Planting his feet apart, his arms clasped behind him, he copied the bland indifference he saw on Edward's face. His brother was astride a horse caparisoned for a festival.

Somerset was first. They'd had to drag him from the abbey. He'd screamed then. Several of his captains had died. Two, who'd coughed blood, still lay lifeless at the foot of the altar. The abbot, wringing his hands, had protested they'd have to reconsecrate the abbey. Edward hadn't bothered to answer.

Richard admired the bold stride with which Somerset marched to the hastily constructed block. He was still in armour, except for his helmet. A handsome man. Calmly he forgave the executioner, then knelt, prayed and waited.

The axe fell gashing the side of his neck. The duke moaned, a convulsion shook him. Blood began to drip onto the cobblestones and form tiny rivulets. In fury the executioner swung again, cleaving the duke's scalp so the axe slid off in a mire of hair and gore. Richard felt sick. Where had they ever gotten such a headsman! Propably a felon winning a pardon for this service. Somerset's body shook with spasms. Dark blood gushed from his mouth.

Several people in the crowd cheered. A good show. By God, it might take three or even four hacks. And there were fourteen men to die.

Richard walked over to the block and handed the headsman a silver coin. "I'll double that if you finish him in one stroke."

The headsman blinked. Through his black hood he recognized the Duke of Gloucester. His bow scraped the ground. He raised the axe, brought it slowly, carefully down and pushed, grating and sawing, through the vital column of the neck. Somerset twisted, groaned. Finally his mangled head fell, lips drawn back in agony.

Fourteen to go. Richard realized his clothes were already spattered with blood. He glanced at Edward. His older brother stared into the far distance. Clarence dipped a handkerchief in the blood. "A little gift for the bitch of Anjou," he laughed. The crowd cheered him and dipped rags, too.

Richard came again to the manor in the evening. He'd washed, changed, even slept a little, but the day was still with him. He wanted Anne to hold him in her arms till all else faded. Joan welcomed him. Anne would be down in a minute. "An' pretty as a love-song," she chuckled. The young duke chatted with Stephen about saddles, especially an ornate new one the leather-master was designing for ladies' palfreys. He met Harriet's young man, Walter Dawson, who'd fought in Hasting's vanguard near the Swillbrook that morning. Walt was apprenticed to the town's leading ironmonger and had two more months to serve. "And then you'll marry?" Richard asked, forcing himself to relax. Not everyone died at the block or in battle.

Harried giggled. "Father and St Venus willing. And the stars right."

Richard thought ahead. The moon ruled early July. A good sign. "I'll send you a wedding-gift."

Harriet gasped. A wedding-gift from the Duke of Gloucester. Better than heaven. She'd brag to all the town.

Richard unwrapped a small package he'd been holding. "And for you, Dame." He held up an assortment of bright ribbons a squire had purchased. "For your gowns."

Joan curtsied. "Your grace is like your brother. Everyone loves him, and so it will be with you."

Richard smiled though the comparison with Edward warmed him. He found Stephen Oldenhall's house a place of comfort, of ease. No tensions lurked here. No fork-tongued Woodville mocked. He hoped he could stay away from the court as the wheel of his life turned. He and Anne.

She came slowly, almost shyly, down the handsome staircase. She was dressed in pale yellow. Full skirts, rustled and billowed below the high waistline, swaying as she walked. Her hair shined as white-gold, plaited and bound with ribbons and buttercups. He could see the glow of her skin, smell the jasmine perfume. "Could my lady and I have a small parlour to ourselves?"

Stephen Oldenhall waved them toward the left wing. The privacy his house afforded was his greatest pride. He could have accommodated all the lovers in Tewkesbury.

Richard embraced Anne in the cool dim light of the small solar. "I'd forgotten how beautiful you are. I wanted to bring a gift. I couldn't find anything. It's been a long day." He didn't add he'd seen enough blood flowing to fill the rivers of Tewkesbury. He sat down beside Anne on a bench backed by pillows against the wall. He noticed the parquet floor. Oldenhall had given them most luxurious rooms.

"Did they find Margaret?"

"She's somewhere in the Malvern Hills. I'm not sure she knows about her son."

Anne nodded. "I hope I never see her again."

"Sweeting, you won't. Listen, I talked to Edward. Briefly. He's not set against you. Today he's angry. I know him. Give him a few days. He'll come round."

"Can you stay with me till he does?" Anne looked up at the dark blue eyes. She willed herself to forget the past year. Only he was real. His square jaw with passionate mouth, the intensity of his gaze, the muscled power of his body and the tenderness of those Plantagenet eyes.

"I don't know, Anne. Plans are still unsettled."

"Take me with you wherever you go."

Richard drew her to him. Her skin was creamy, smooth. He wanted to hold her forever. Under his kiss her lips opened warm and responding. "Anne, I'll try. God. I'll try." He caressed her breast and felt her stiffen, draw back slightly.

"Sweeting, what's wrong?"

"I don't know." A sick misery gripped her mind. "There's been so much pain. I know you'd never hurt me."

Richard thought of the dead Prince. He looked like a boy lying in the abbey on view for the gawkers. Much of his hair had been snipped away for trophies till Edward had posted a guard. That accursed brute must have hurt Anne terribly. His little Anne.

He kissed her gently and forced a smile. "We needn't hurry. We've a lifetime."

Anne touched his hair. "And you'll weave me flower crowns again? Ah, Richard, you are my life."

He held her. "Let time heal, my little one. And sleep, good food. It has not been a day."

"Yet we're together." Anne didn't want to think, just be.

II

"No! No! No!" Edward's face was softer than his words.
"The little Neville's not ready in any case. A wounded bird,
Dick."

"And you think her wounds will heal with Clarence
nearby."

"She'll have Isabel. A sister to confide in. Time to forget.
George will be busy with his own schemes. He always is."

"Edward, let me marry her. Here. Take her with me."

"Here. Besides the rotting corpse of her last husband.
Brother, you're Constable and Admiral of England. You
must be my power in the North. The Scots are restless, as
usual. The Devil knows what Percy's up to. You're already
Warden of the West Marches. I'm giving you authority over
the East and Middle Marches. Percy will be in your
hands." He paused, studied his brother's face. "Also Sheriff
Hutton and Middleham." He turned on his heel, shouted
back. "North, Dick. Show those mad Scots who rules
England again. Stop at Middleham if you like."

Richard watched him go. He probably was right. Anne
needed time to heal. Isabel would take care of her. And he'd
have Middleham. Home.

Anne miserably remembered Richard's farewell as George of Clarence, her brother-in-law, showed her about his refurbished London mansion. She'd been so happy those three days. Too happy. Perhaps such joy was a fey thing. She knew too she hadn't been able to hide her unexpected hesitation when Richard embraced her. Pain had been part of a man's touch for too long. She hated herself for letting it show.

"This place was built for giants." George, tall but not muscular, loomed over her. "Old Salisbury used to house five hundred men with their horses here and in the grounds."

Anne glanced around The Erber. "It's immense," she agreed. "Where are we in London?"

"In Downgate near Thames Streets. In one of the great houses. For the great." George added without self-consciousness.

He kept a firm grip on his sister-in-law. "You're a prisoner, you know." He thought with a little luck the attainder might never be lifted. Then this chit couldn't inherit. All the riches would be Isabel's.

"I know. Where's Isabel?" Ridiculous to fear this shallow man, she told herself. To fear at all since Richard loved her and promised to take her to Middleham.

"She'll be here soon. You must keep to your room, Anne. You're a traitor's daughter. Widow of an enemy. I'm being kind to take you in."

"George, I'll not run away."

He smirked. "No, be assured you will not. I do this kindness for Isabel. You could be in the Tower. Chained."

"I understand."

George waved a ringed hand. "Your room's up the back stairs. I'll send Isabel to you."

Anne glanced at her brother-in-law. The lines of his face

were hard, like the King's. She said only, "I've missed my sister."

Isabel came in the afternoon. "George wanted you to have a chance to, well, settle in a bit after the ride from Tewkesbury. I'm sorry the room is so small. He insisted." Suddenly she hugged Anne like they were both still children. "My dear, has it been so terrible? Everyone said it was a brutal and treacherous business. Even the statesmen. George told me."

Anne looked at Isabel thoughtfully. Her sister had filled out. Her beautiful skin glowed with improved health. She wore appleblossom silk all fluffed with lace.

"It was as they say, Isabel." Anne answered slowly. She had to be careful. Isabel loved her husband. "It's over."

Isabel looked away. "George says if you were not my sister ..." She thought of George, drunk and angry, swearing he could have killed Anne at Tewkesbury. "Harebrained hoyden. Came right on the field," he'd mumbled and the cup had crashed to the floor.

"It was Richard who took care of me, Isabel. I stayed at a fine manor. I've never seen such comfort. Afterwards, Richard had to go to Scotland at the King's bidding. Border uprisings as usual. So I thank George and you." Anne didn't want to talk about George of Clarence, his duplicity, his harshness. "Is Ankarette with you?"

"Oh yes. She's been wonderful. Such a comfort. You'll see. Anne, I prayed for you each day."

Anne smiled and patted Isabel's arm. "And here I am."

It was Ankarette who brought water to wash and some gowns from Isabel's wardrobe. The servant was stouter, ruddier. "When does the Duke of Gloucester return from Scotland?" she asked bluntly. The girl needed protection. Much as she loved Isabel, Ankarette disliked and mistrusted George of Clarence. She was sure he'd plot something, anything, to keep all the inheritance.

"I don't know," Anne answered slowly. "While Richard's north he plans to stop at Middleham and Sheriff Hutton. Those estates of my father have been ceded to him." The names were a joy to say.

Ankarette nodded. "Don't talk about estates to Clarence, Anne. He wants it all. Beauchamp, Salisbury, Warwick – every bit."

"Clarence never liked the North."

"He likes being very rich."

"And Isabel?"

"Oh, your sister is unaware. She knows he claims land as her husband, as is natural. She doesn't bother about the extent of it. That you are entitled to half she would readily accept, if asked. No one asks."

Anne understood. "Clarence would like me to vanish somehow. Just fade into a nunnery, say."

"Exactly."

The girl grinned at Ankarette. "I'm no nun."

"And the Duke of Gloucester isn't a monk."

Anne looked at her broken nails. She could feel her ribs through the dress. "I must get pretty again, Ankarette. For Richard."

"You will, dear lady." Ankarette plied the comb. "I'll see to it. Time and God heal."

Within the week, Isabel's dresses no longer hung on Anne like sacks. Studying her with the critical perusal of an older sister, Isabel found no fault. It was hard though to think of Anne as a woman.

Isabel returned to her mirror and with a slender finger pushed at the thin arch of her eyebrow. "Uncle George, still Archbishop of York, may come by, Anne. The twitching hypocrite."

Anne thought of her youngest uncle. His dexterity was amazing. He always landed on the winning side.

"What happened to John Fortescue?" She knew all the military leaders were dead. She'd wondered about the man who'd tried to be kind.

"Oh, he's harmless. He and Dr Morton are in prison. 'Tis said Fortescue will soon be free and serving as a lawyer. He swears his loyalty to England."

"Margaret?" Anne found it difficult to say the name.

"She fled across the Avon but they caught her. Sir William Stanley found her at Little Malvery Priory. She's in the Tower.

"It doesn't matter, Isabel. Margaret won't struggle now her son is dead."

Isabel nodded. "Obviously or else she'd be dead too. Everyone wanted to see her head roll. I've heard she's a hag."

"And King Henry? The Tower?"

"Executed. Didn't I tell you they're all dead." Isabel spoke with detachment. Her mind didn't dwell in the past. She wished George would come to bed sober and she'd conceive. Angels and cupids were woven into their new bed-hangings.

"Richard is Constable of England. He's in charge of executions?"

"Yes, Anne," Isabel turned from the mirror. "I'm having a dress made, a deep blue with slashes of silver. Would you like a gown for Richard's return? Blue is good with your hair and eyes."

"I don't know, Isabel." Her hands were locked so the knuckles shown white. "I become numbed when I think back. I feel so degraded, soiled."

Isabel put her arm about her sister. "Didn't Richard take

care of you after Tewkesbury? He knows you need time to recover. He said he wouldn't forsake you, so he'll come. Don't you realize, Anne," and a note of unusual bitterness prevailed in Isabel's voice, "when Richard vows it is forever."

III

It was in the formal rose-garden, seated on a stone bench, where the sun warmed their faces, that Archbishop Uncle George found his two nieces. He was wrapped in velvet though the day was warm and humid. The edge of his stole was enriched with embroidery of slanted crosses, his amice was snowy-white, from his shoulders a gold and crystal cross blinked in the light as it swung on a heavy chain.

"Good-morrow, your grace." Isabel curtsied.

"God be with you, niece." His left eye twitched. "And how do you these summer days, Anne? I wouldn't have recognized you. You have greatly changed."

She too curtsied. "For the better I hope, Uncle."

"Yes, I suppose. That dress is a bit festive for a widow. I thought to find you in mourning." His dismay increased. God, it was hot! The girl looked stubborn as a mule.

Anne wondered fleetingly why this brother had survived and Uncle John was dead. "I mourned my father when he was alive. Now he rests in peace. My husband ... I did what I could."

"Dear niece, you've hardened your heart, as is natural, against a cruel world. Wouldn't you be happiest in a convent where wordly cares would never again intrude?"

Anne watched the slight tick in his left eyelid quicken as he spoke. She was sure Clarence had sent him.

"You're so kind, Uncle. However, I haven't the least desire to enter a convent."

"You can't mean to return to society, Anne. You've no land, indeed nothing but the charity of Isabel."

"And to that she is most welcome." Isabel regarded the archbishop blandly. "My husband tells me he hopes to secure both the Neville properties and my mother's Beauchamp estates. If the lands do not revert to the crown, isn't Anne entitled to half? In which case you can hardly call her a charity."

The eyelid was in full flicker now. "My dear Isabel. What do you know of legal matters? Any small grants of land can be donated to the convent. It's often done by widows."

"By old widows." Anne said sweetly.

"My dear niece, I do but advise. A surrogate father, if you will." The thought of Clarence's adamant orders made his stomach churn.

Anne smiled. "No, dear Uncle."

Later, in the quiet of the night, Anne decided though her churchly uncle spoke for Clarence he'd not speak too harshly. He'd balance all sides. No reward hid in a plan which pitted him against Richard as Constable of England. Executions were so easy to order. He'd not push. Anne wished she could dream of Richard and some future. She was glad though her dreams were finally free of dead faces.

Standing beside the giant massiveness of the Tower on the Galley Quay, Anne looked up river at the pride of the city – London Bridge. She couldn't have imagined it. "It's so big."

Isabel nodded. "Immense. Nineteen arches and a drawbridge. See the hodge-podge of homes and shops? I always think they're going to slide right off into the Thames.''

Anne swallowed. "All those heads on pikes." She could see rags of dead flesh, melted eyes. She turned back to the river. Dozens of tiny boats darted back and forth, like restless minnows, carrying passengers to the opposite side for a pence. Everywhere men, some richly dressed, called, "Wagge, wagge! Go we hence," and the more costly their garment the quicker a boatman and his wherry appeared. Heavy merchant galleys moved in stately procession, ignoring the small boats criss-crossing their paths. The sharp aroma of salted codfish drifted on the air from Billingsgate. Fishermen caught smelts, salmon, pike and flounder from the same pier on which they waited. It was so alive, the odours, the noise, the commotion. Paris was said to be four times as large as London, but that city was as grey as winter skies. Here all was bright with colour. Anne shaded her eyes and strained to see up river.

"Isabel. The royal barges! Oh, so beautiful!''

Isabel nodded. "Six of them. A procession.''

They watched as the floating giants of carved wood, sailed toward the Galley Quay. Canopied with striped silk, garlanded and trailing wind-caught pennants, the barges were more lovely than the white swans swimming in high-necked arrogance around them.

"All this for us?'' Anne wondered.

"I don't know.'' Isabel was uneasy.

Anne, George and Isabel had been summoned to this royal outing by invitation from the King. They were to travel as far as Windsor by barge, a long journey. George had sworn at first that they'd not go. "I've no stomach for ships,'' he'd said peevishly, staring at the parchment from which dangled the royal seal. "And why must we bring Anne? I see no reason.''

Isabel had put her head on his shoulder and stroked his cheek. "No doubt the King thinks to honour you in being gracious toward your sister-in-law," she had murmured. Now as the boats drew close Isabel watched puzzled. Anger flushed George's face.

The royal barge stopped at the quay. King Edward himself came ashore to greet them. The wind blew a piece of hair across Anne's forehead and caught at her skirts. The King was so tall, she didn't even come to his shoulder. Her curtsy was half greeting, half trembling.

"Welcome, Lady Anne." He had a soft wooing way. Very different from at Tewkesbury. "Back to England, to London, to life." And to love and a warm bed, he added mentally, thinking her a sweetmeat for any night.

She looked up at him. His hair was golden in the sun. Pearl and diamonds blazed as sun and roses in his linked collar.

"I am happy, very happy, to be in England, your grace."

"You still look like a girl. Delightful. Enchanting." He broke off. "You must meet my wife. Isabel, George, you're both well?" He barely glanced at them.

"Damn him to Hell." George's curse carried on the summer air. "Are we to ride with the Queen on this tedious journey? He knows I can't abide ...."

"Hush." Isabel cautioned. "We'll sort it out."

Queen Elizabeth Woodville, assisted by several gentleman, had stepped lightly out of the barge. She felt every day of her thirty-six years. Six years older than her stud-husband, she knew the effort it took to convey the impression time simply passed her by, leaving her beautiful and untouched. No lines of happiness or sorrow etched her finely boned face with its small mouth and high, white forehead. She held out a ring-laden hand for Anne to kiss.

"Anne Neville," she said in flat tones. "Welcome." And a bane on you, she thought with rancour. Vile, no doubt, like all the Nevilles.

Anne curtsied deeply. She was wary of Elizabeth Woodville. The Queen's eyebrows plucked to a thin line lifted slightly.

"I hope you've renounced your foul past."

She made it sound a lifetime of evil. Vaguely Anne wondered how she kept her elaborate gauze hairdress from blowing in the wind. White blonde hair was pulled tightly back. Anne answered slowly, aware the King watched and a wrong word could put her in the Tower.

"I cannot renounce what has been. It is done."

Elizabeth Woodville smiled slightly. She fashioned a trap. "And you feel no shame at the grief your kind have brought upon England? And your scapegallows father?" She remembered with a shiver giving birth within Westminster, while Warwick held London. A travail on the rack of vexation.

Anne looked away. She could see a galley unloading bales of damask and soft velvet nearby. Further along the great cranes of London were swinging bales of incoming commodities from ship to wharf. Her life as a free person must have hung as precariously as the burden on those cranes. "I regret," she began, "it's not just regret, it is sorrow this past year happened."

Elizabeth Woodville acknowledged this with a slight wave of her perfumed hand. "And your penance? Knees raw with kneeling, head shaved in grief for the rest of your life, might somewhat atone." She wished she could order it.

Anne felt desperate. The Woodville Queen was without mercy. Enmity was her very nature. Anne knelt before the King, dimly aware of many watching. "Your grace, I love

England, and I accept you as the anointed King. With all my heart. What more do you want of me?"

Edward quickly lifted the girl up. "Little cousin, that is enough." A faint tenderness softened his face. "Richard has asked many times for permission to marry you. You may tell him it is granted."

She was startled. "Richard! He's here? Oh, don't tease me."

Edward laughed. "Cousin, never before have I gone to such lengths to arrange a glad meeting. Usually I leave such pleasantries to the ladies. But my youngest brother is very persistent these days. I've had no peace since he returned from Scotland."

"Richard is here?"

Edward nodded. "A splendid setting for delight. A fine September day, all London around you, minstrels, refreshments, a barge festooned in green. It's the third one and will dock when we pull away." Still smiling the King turned to Isabel and Clarence. "You're to go on the fourth barge with Will Hasting. Your travel coffers can be accommodated there, too. We'll talk again at Windsor."

George's red face had become splotchy. "Anne's in mourning, brother. This is not fitting."

It was easy to see why people loved Edward. His laughter was warm, boyish. "George, you're so obvious. Anne looks about as mournful as a wild rose. And even lovelier. Don't you agree, wife?"

Elizabeth Woodville had resumed her cushioned seat in the barge. "A wild rose for Gloucester and how much land for Clarence? A pretty problem." She smiled and tiny teeth briefly showed. "Or a dung-heap."

The Queen enjoyed seeing brothers fight and didn't trouble to hide it. Elizabeth Woodville was a great power.

Since she'd borne the King a son, no one would ever cross her.

Edward laughed again. Clarence swore, but not loudly. Isabel pressed her sister's hand. "A happy meeting, Anne. We'll see you at Windsor."

IV

The third barge. He stood near the front and Anne waved as the boat pulled up to the quay. Fleetingly, she tried to be demure, to wait quietly as Richard stepped to the pier. Then, forgetting everyone else, she half-ran toward him, skirts pulling at her ankles, the little cap of seed-pearls slipping back on her head.

"Anne." He drew the girl toward him. Just their hands entwined and the river, the barges, the very city, became but a dim background. He touched her hair; hard gentleness coursed through him as his arm encircled her waist. "More beautiful than my memories." His lips sought hers.

Anne lifted her face to him. The days at Tewkesbury had not prepared her for this Richard. Then he had been tired, dressed in work clothes. Today he was a prince of the realm with green showing in the slashings of his sleeves and a brooch of diamonds and emeralds set in his velvet cap. Beneath the festive clothing his young, agile body exuded steely strength.

"It doesn't seem possible, Richard. Here. Together."

Her voice faltered. "Ah, let's not talk about it."

He helped her into the barge and led her to a cushioned seat, secluded from the rest of the boat by a curtain of brocade and velvet and sheltered overhead by a gold-tasseled canopy. Anne leaned against him and the trembling in her heart began to quiet. She'd no longer stand alone in a violent world. Love was here to stand beside her.

Richard called to the minstrels at the front of the boat and they began to play the lively Pas de Brebant, a dance tune, blending pipe and tabor, lute and harp and bells. The lilting notes drifted back while, like a gaint water-flower, the barge moved up the Thames following the bend of the river toward Westminster. Great warehouses boarded both sides. The aroma of spices, a blend of cloves and nutmeg, drifted from a Venetian galley. At another wharf a Flemish carvel discharged Holland cloth and a fine ship from Spain rode low in the river, heavy with its cargo of wood and iron and oil. The white swans still followed, hoping for handouts. A tiny wherry crossed their path and an overstout gentleman so loaded it down he was repeatedly dunked. His howls of protest to his indifferent boatman mingled with the music of the minstrels.

Anne laughed and leaned back in Richard's arms. "It's real. The blue sky, the smell of fish, the sound of bells, you. I've lived so long on dreams." Her hand rested on his shoulder. "Tell me what we are seeing, Richard. I don't know London town."

Richard kissed her lightly. "Oh, a King and a Queen, some swans, an ugly bulk of buildings called Steelyard owned by the short-tempered merchants of the Hanse, and a duke who sees nothing but you."

"Surely you see the cranes," she teased. "They're giants."

"The best. Would the vintner spoil a tun, a drop, of their Bordeaux wine? Let's see if their wine is worthy of today."

Anne nodded and in a moment a squire appeared with two goblets and a tray of tiny meat-pies, fruits and cheeses.

"There, just beyond Charing Cross, is Westminster Palace and the Abbey. I think London's soul is in the Abbey. It's a glorious place. I must take you there sometime, my love." He smiled down at her. "Sweeting, your eyes are dreamy. Am I such a poor guide?"

"I was just listening to your voice," she confessed. "I wish time could stand still. This day forever."

"Yes." Richard was suddenly pensive.

"Is George being troublesome? He's a rascal, you know. Your brother the King was most gracious. The Queen, well ..." Anne spread her hands in a shrug. "George boils with choler, Richard. I think he was born so."

"He would take all your inheritance. I'll not let him. Jupiter may be entering Virgo and the sun be in its first house. I'll still not abjure your birthright."

Richard made it of little consequence, but there was a hard undercurrent. He put down his wine. "Anne, we've so little time. When I thought I'd lost you a part of me died, or so it seemed. To have to fight your father – I didn't want that, ever. This is our moment. I feel it. I wouldn't rush you, but we have this hour, this day. The future is always unknown. I've asked the King's permission to marry you."

"And he told me to tell you," she took a deep breath, "it is granted."

"Oh, thank God – and Edward." Richard pulled her to him; his muscular, leanness pressed against the soft silk of her dress. It was as though she'd never been kissed before. Her lips parted under his, they tasted the wine of each other's mouths. She knew her breasts were hard, eager, beneath his caress. "Sweeting, we must marry soon. Anne, you're all I've ever wanted."

He drew her to him so their heads rested on a single pillow, hair mingling. "Anne, sweetheart, listen. I was at Middleham but a few days ago. Nothing has changed, even the wild flowers on the moors bloom as before. It's home, Anne, but only if you're there. I want to go back, away from court and all the Woodvilles and political games. I want to take you home, Anne. As my wife."

She watched him as he spoke, seeing the intense blue of his eyes, the high Plantagenet cheekbones, the ardent line of his mouth. So she had envisioned him, now she could touch his face. "Richard, why do we linger here?"

They both laughed. Richard kissed her joyfully. "The papal dispensation can be arranged by your own uncle. I'll settle these land matters. Within a week, Anne, it should take no longer." He kissed her on the nose, the top of her head, the curve of her breasts.

"Richard," Anne clung to him laughing, "you were never so impetuous as a boy."

He looked at her in mock solemnness. "And where's that shy little girl I used to know?"

The white swans followed the royal barges all the way up the Thames to Windsor, their number increasing as the riverway grew narrower and the water more gentle. In the early evening Windsor was alight with the western sun slanting across it, a giant mass of crenelated towers and walls set in a frame of green fields. The town hid behind the castle, but there were a few colourful tents pitched upon the greensward near the river and even at a distance there was an air of activity as gaily dressed people moved about like gaudy figurines. A trumpet-call of York Herald marked the end of the voyage. Pages, squires and servants raced from the castle.

Richard smiled at her reassuringly. "Windsor's a

friendly castle, Anne, not so proud as it looks. I think you'll find all to your liking here."

"It's beautiful." She stirred lazily in his arms. "Not dismal like so many Norman buildings."

"Well, my little one, the Normans were building fortresses on the whole. They didn't trust the local population." Richard grinned. "Can't say I blame them. The Anglo-Saxons were a butchering lot. To say nothing of the Celts. But Windsor was begun as a hunting-lodge, a place of pleasure. The game's still plentiful in the forest. Everyone is always in a festive mood here, even, I hope, Clarence."

Anne straightened up reluctantly, smoothing back her hair. "See George has a prominent seat at the high table, flatter him, act as though his whims are serious. He wants to be taken seriously."

"I know." Richard dusted crumbs from both their clothes. "Edward has given him honours and awards, a long list."

"Honeyed pastry would taste bitter to Clarence," Anne said slowly, licking her own fingers. "I give him to your care, Richard. I can't worry when I feel so happy."

Richard kissed her quickly as they docked. "You look magical, Anne. Could you say a few witching words and transport my rogue brother to Cathay, or even Avalon?"

She laughed. "I'll try. The very next time I remember to bring my potions and wand." She saw the mists of evening had begun to encircle the taller of the castle towers. "Clarence has a dark side. I don't think we know his mind. But Isabel loves him. He must have virtues."

"Sweeting, of course. Worry became a habit this past year. No more now that you're safe." Richard stepped onto the pier and lifted the girl after him. Anne stayed in his arms a moment longer than necessary before walking toward the tower-bordered Inner Gateway which led to the Middle Ward of Windsor Castle.

V

Cicely Neville, Plantagenet and Duchess of York by
marriage, pointed a bony finger at her eldest son. "Dolt,
you've thrown your cousin to the wolves. They'll eat her
alive."

"Second cousin." Edward answered mildly. He had
struggled for years to keep straight his mother's many
relations. Daughter of Ralph Neville, she was the youngest
of twenty-three children. Her oldest brother had been
Warwick's father. Born near Durham she now lived in
considerable splendour at Fotheringhay. He'd not expected
her.

"Anne's not a child," he added, wishing she'd leave him
alone. He liked Windsor especially his luxurious private
chambers. His newly refurbished bedroom had a portable
night-stool, a private terrace and a mirror among the bed-
curtains.

"I thought merely to give Richard and his little Anne a
holiday. Dick's hot for the girl." He sighed. His mother
wasn't nearly finished.

"So then, that child and Richard can marry tomorrow?"

"Well, not exactly." Edward squirmed, thought of a hot
bath, his squires scraping him down till he felt fresh and

tingly. "They've got to have a dispensation, of course. And Clarence wants every inch of land. I'd like to keep George happy, but I'll not cheat Richard. It will take some working out, I suppose."

"George isn't easily gulled." Cicely was thoughtful. "And you're a great ninny." She smiled at her favourite son, her handsome, lazy Edward. Naturally, he'd thought no further.

She held up a freckled hand. "The Woodvilles." One finger bent. "They'll hate her for being Warwick's daughter." A second finger snapped. "Clarence wants her out of the way, somehow, anyhow, so he can take all the inheritance. Buckingham is here. He's a strange one. He's been fawning after Richard since you returned. He'll not like a diddling girl in his way." Her thumb closed about her hand. She jerked upward the one stiff finger. "And that to your court. Protect Anne."

Edward closed his eyes. "She and Richard will be at supper tonight, Mother. Talk to them."

"Oh, I'll talk. Don't I always?" She hesitated a moment. "George was such a lovely baby. Sometimes I'm afraid for him, too." Cicely gathered her full skirts about her. "If only anyone listened."

Edward watched her go with relief. He thought fondly that mothers were impossible. Yet he had to admit shrewd. He shrugged and yelled for his squires.

In the solar assigned to Anne, a brown-haired girl stood by the door and curtsied.

"I'm Anne Fitz Hugh, daughter of Lord Henry Fitz Hugh, and I'm down from Oxford to be with my betrothed, Francis Lovell. Everyone calls me Nan." She said it all in one breath.

Anne, awed by the tremendous size and beauty of Windsor, was startled. "I knew Francis Lovell when he trained at Middleham. We were children together."

"I know, my lady. Francis speaks often of those days."
Nan smiled without rancour. "If Francis were a poet, you'd
be the lady of his poems."

Anne blushed, but saw the idea bothered this happy-
faced girl not at all. "Francis remembers me as a child. Will
he be at dinner?"

Nan Fitz Hugh nodded. "Oh, everyone will be there. The
Duke of Gloucester has the whole palace jumping because
of you. The gleemen you hear have been practising for
days." Nan picked up a mirror and quickly set to rights her
own hair and dress. "Windsor is crowded. I think they will
house guests in the prison cells soon." Nan went to a
draped rack, pulled aside a covering cloth and held out a
dress of creamy silk, the neckline wrought in delicate green
leaves interwined with hearts and powdered with tiny
jewels. "Do you like it, my lady? The duke told me to have
the very best made for you, so I did."

Anne pressed a piece of cool silk to her cheek. "It's
beautiful. How was there time? How did you know my
size?"

Nan laughed. "Plantagenet men order things done, like
that." She snapped her fingers. "We gambled you'd wear
the same size as the Lady Isabel, and her dressmaker is very
chatty. But we must hurry."

With quick nimbleness Nan helped her change, adjusted
the low shoulder-line, pulled in the waist. "Now for some
cochineal paste for a blush."

Anne felt rather wanton and realized with amazement
she enjoyed the feeling. "It is so low, Nan."

Nan laughed. "And you with not a freckle on your
shoulders. Even lower would be perfect." She combed
Anne's hair long and loose and sprinkled jasmine perfume
on the girl's bare shoulders.

"Everyone will look at me."

"Of course. You're a bit of a legend already. A story with a happy ending." She clapped her hands. "I almost forgot. Jewels too from your lover, forgive me, his grace, the Duke of Gloucester." She opened a box lined in velvet and Anne saw a gold filigree collar with the letters R and A intertwined.

"You like it?" Nan fastened the collar. "A tiring-woman was supposed to be here. I can't imagine what keeps her. I'm afraid we'll be late. Oh, St Serverus, the hat! There's the supper horn."

"My hat?" Anne looked in amazement at the tall, pointed headdress with the veil of silver tissue which Nan Fitz Hugh held out. "Will it stay on?"

"Oh yes, it's all the fashion. From Burgundy, I believe. The princess style." Nan worked busily with hairpins and the arrangement of the veil, then again held up the mirror. "See!"

Anne touched the folds of the dress, the delicate collar and the towering headdress. Gifts of love. It had been a long time. "To dinner then, Nan."

"Holy Saints, yes."

Most of the guests were already present by the time they made their way to the Great Hall at Windsor. Tonight every recess of the stone vaulting was lit by torches and candles. The air was heavy with the scent of spices, rich food and flowers. The King, already seated under a canopy at the high table on the dias, had joined his minstrels in a ribald song. Servants scurried about with great platters of meat in thick sauces and flagons of wine and mead. Many of lesser rank had seated themselves at lower tables, running perpendicular to the King's table, and they were squeezed closely together on one side so the other might be free for service.

Anne stood for a moment, hesitating, then realized that the squire who had just bowed before her was requesting he be allowed to conduct her to the head table. She smiled at Nan and followed the squire, very conscious of the glow of the cream silk and her bare shoulders, aware too of the whispers and craning of necks. St Agnes, let the hat stay on, she thought and held her head high. She curtsied before the King and Queen while Edward smiled and the Queen tore at bits of white bread.

"You look most fair, cousin." Edward grinned wider. "And so very young. It makes us here all feel the weight of our years." Anne saw the Queen choke on a piece of bread and gulp wine. Edward didn't appear to notice. "Gloucester," he called, "you best claim your lady else all the gentlemen will be asking for her favour."

Richard was by her side in a moment. "I do so claim." His ducal coronet gleamed against his dark hair, tonight he was like flame in blue and gold. He put her hand through the bend of his arm and escorted her to a place beside him at the high table. Somehow in that Great Hall he filled Anne's whole vision. Never had he looked handsomer, more sure of himself. She realized with a start he was performing various introductions.

The young man on her left was Henry Stafford, Duke of Buckingham, married to the Queen's sister, Katherine. Buckingham was about her own age and uneasy. His hands drummed on the table. He kept glancing at the Queen. Her sister his wife, Katherine Woodville, sitting two places down, looked like a frog in pale green. Toad, turd, trull, trollop. The rhythm of the words pleased him. His mind silently shouted the epithets. How surprised the whey-faced Woodvilles would be if they knew his mind, Buckingham thought.

"And on my right," went on Richard, pointing with his

fork, "is the Bishop of Lincoln, Thomas Rotherham." He pointed around the bishop's stiff back. "There's the Queen's sister, Mary, in silver silk, and William Herbert, the Young Earl of Pembroke, and, of course, Clarence and Isabel ..." He stopped seeing she was looking down the Hall.

"Yes, it's Francis Lovell, sweeting." Richard smiled at his friend. "Were you surprised to find you shared a solar with his betrothed? I meant to tell you on the barge, but I forgot. It seems I could think of only one thing."

Anne dipped a piece of partridge in sweet sauce. "Richard, you remembered well enough to make this like my saint's day when I was a child. The dress, the jewels. And the gleemen. We must have music at Middleham." She thought of how Richard had protected her, cherished her, and not just today. She smiled at him. "It will take me all my life to thank you."

Richard lifted his glass. "To our lifetime together, Anne. Until we are old and grey and creak. Even that will not be long enough."

VI

It was late into the banquet when a trumpet blew interrupting all conversation. Everyone turned to the door while a herald shouted that Lady Cicely of Raby, Duchess of York, entered; and "Proud Cis", as she was generally called, enveloped in velvet, ermine and the heavy scent of musk, walked with quick steps to her eldest son. Anne saw her exchange greeting with Edward, nod briefly at George and Isabel and come their way.

"Best make room, sweeting," Richard sighed. "My lady mother's going to join us."

Anne eased her chair closer to Buckingham and pulled her skirts about her ankles.

"If you please, Madame, and the King will give me leave," Buckingham rose and bowed formally towards Cicely, "you may have my place. I'd be honoured."

Surprisingly, Buckingham's voice was pleasantly mellow. His pinched, restless face suggested emotions only partially held in check. Women everywhere, Buckingham thought. He hated them all. He wished Richard had given him a brotherly hug as he sometimes did. No point in hoping for Richard even if he were the passive partner. He remembered the page-boy, all pink and tender-skinned, waiting in his apartment. The boy would sing sweetly first. Buckingham hurried through the torch-lit corridors. The chance to leave had been heaven-sent.

Cicely took her place. She was used to having her own way. Her own court at Fotheringhay was totally centred around her whim. Without further notice of Buckingham, she faced her niece. "Welcome to court, Anne Neville."

The girl politely kissed the rough skin of Cicely's hand. "Thank you, Madame." Anne recalled Cicely was proud of her Neville descent, as she was proud of everything.

Cicely heaped her plate high with food, including swan, peacock, plover, several small blackbirds, and other meats too covered with pastry shells to be identified. The duchess had such a bony frame. A wonder she could eat so much. While she devoured the mound of food, Cicely bluntly examined her niece, until Anne flushed.

Richard tried to bridge the pause. "I've not seen you in many months, Mother. All's well at Fotheringhay?"

"Oh, well enough." Cicely wiped her mouth with a heavy linen napkin which she tossed to the squire who stood beside her. "I decided to come and see for myself your choice of wife, Dick." She patted Anne's cheek. "You look a bit delicate, my dear, but I like your face. Childbirth will fill you out."

Cicely laughed loudly. "Though a full bevy of seven healthy babes, and five dead ones too, did nothing for me. Well, Richard, marry the lass and be off to the north before George causes trouble. I saw him just now. He thrives on trouble. One day his charm will fail to get him out of it."

"I hope not to anger George," Richard spoke evenly.

Anne looked from mother to youngest son and thought there was much she didn't know. Richard was deeply worried about George of Clarence and so was his mother. She saw Queen Elizabeth break off a chunk of the Round

Tower from a 'soteltie' and the King in animated conversation with Will Hastings.

Cicely followed her glance. "Hastings, as Lord Chamberlain, is in charge of all this, Anne."

"I see, Madame, and he is the King's true friend?"

Cicely shrugged. Her fingers tapped impatiently on the table. Suddenly she explained in low, staccato bursts. "Everyone knows. Even the Queen. Why not you? With the help of this friend Hastings, my son has sunk in a few weeks from magnificent leader of York to prowling stud. He's tired of the Queen. She's alienated all his true friends. He's weary, too, of the Woodville family and their everlasting clamour for power and money and responsibility for which they're not fit. They owe him everything, but they whine and beg for more. And in an exigency they slink away to places of safety. A pity your father didn't execute more than the bitch Queen's father and one brother. No charges were led by Woodvilles at Barnet or Tewkesbury. God rest the souls of your father and his brother, John Neville. At least they didn't hide from death."

Anne took a deep breath and looked away. "But there will be peaceful years ahead, Madame. The King has a fine young son."

"Oh aye, peace, but it comes too late for Edward. Too many deaths and betrayals to remember. He's more man than King. God pity him."

Richard leaned across to his mother. "Edward will be healed of his disillusionments. Wait, in time. When all are loyal."

Cicely rubbed her neck, which had turned red with emotion. "You're too young, Richard, to know about disillusionments. It's you who will see." Her beautiful children, she thought sadly. They'd all grown and gone.

Anne stared down at her food. She knew some wounds never healed but just scabbed over only to fester and open again. Strange such wounds might be hidden in the heart.

The duchess talked to Richard in her low rasping voice. "The Queen, whose virtue would only be satisfied with a crown, now bores Edward. Perhaps on purpose. He finds life flat and stale. All I see are more mistresses, more hunting, more ceremonial pomp, and more indifference."

"I will be steadfast." Richard spoke the simple words with intensity.

Cicely straightened, her fork resumed its clanging service. "Young," she muttered, her mouth full. "Too young to know."

Anne placed a timid hand on Richard's arm, wondering if she dared change this mood which was draining all sweetness from the evening. "I think the minstrels are playing the Danse au Chapelet. I remember some steps from the dancing master at Middleham."

Richard smiled in relief. Pages were bringing in hand-basins and ewers for washing. The giant 'soteltie' which had once duplicated the whole castle of Windsor was a confusion of bits and pieces. Other food was also being whisked away.

Cicely rapped her son on the hand. "Dance tonight, Dick, but tomorrow take this pretty child and go north." Cicely chuckled and Anne caught a glimpse of the vivacious charm that had once endowed this woman with the name of Rose of Raby.

"Mother, you're right. There's the papal dispensation and the land settlement, but I'm in no mood to wait."

Cicely gulped her wine, suddenly old again. She regarded them both through half-closed eyes. "So listen to me. I'm a weathervane when it comes to your brother

Clarence, and I don't like the way the wind blows." She shut her eyes, precluding any answer. "Dance, dance," she commanded.

Richard led Anne proudly to the centre of the floor. She's the most beautiful of all, he thought. Sweeter than honey. He took her hand in his. "This dance ends with a kiss, you know."

"Yes." Anne bit her lips, then laughed. "Didn't I practically drag you from the table?"

"Every man tonight envied the Duke of Gloucester." Nan Fitz Hugh blew out the candle and settled comfortably under the thick quilts of the bed. It was very late. "A triumphant dancer, all agile grace. And such muscles. The styles are marvellously revealing. And you were his perfect partner, my lady."

Anne fluffed a pillow and sank pleasantly into the darkness. They had danced many rounds, giddy with wine and laughter. Even the Duchess Cicely had tapped her fingers with enjoyment, before dozing off in her chair. At an hour long past her bedtime the King had had his eldest daughter, Elizabeth, brought in for the admiration of the court and the long-legged King had danced a rustic Hey with his pretty and sleepy child. At the end Nan and Francis and Richard and Anne had taken a long, strolling walk back to the solar. Francis had the same steady, candid brown eyes as in boyhood. Richard's friend and a man to trust.

"You and Francis must come to Middleham when we're all married." Anne was half asleep.

"Oh, we will. With babies and baggage-carts."

Anne snuggled down deeper under the covers; the wine was still warm in her blood though not as warm as Richard's kisses. The melodies of the minstrels sang distantly in her head.

VII

"Surely you didn't mean to pardon the Neville brat."
Elizabeth Woodville stretched out lazily in her husband's
bed. A new sheer nightrobe covered her legs, her breasts
were bare. "You've no regard for my feelings. A dead
father ..."

"Some we all have in common." Edward hadn't expected
her. Damn bitch. Double-damn her proud white breasts.
He knew the nipples would turn hard if he touched them.
He could feel the heat in his loins. "Leave Anne Neville
alone, wife. She'll be going North soon."

Elizabeth stretched. "I've had a marvellous idea. If the
crown confiscated all the Neville lands, your brothers
wouldn't quarrel." All that vast wealth. It made her think
of rich brandy. She could order more jewels, new tapestries,
oak panelling for her rooms at Westminster, a musk-ball of
gold with pearls and lace. The list was a long one.

"And how do you propose I'd justify such a seizure?"

Elizabeth shrugged. She remembered stealing the royal
seal and ordering several murders. Anything could be
arranged. It just took some imagination. "Couldn't you
send your brothers off? George has lands in Ireland.
Richard'd go crusading if you asked him. You never see
these things, Edward."

He sat down beside her. The nightgown fell away. He played with her breasts, ruffled her pubic hair. "Love me, Elizabeth?"

"My sweet, I adore you."

Edward smelled her heavy perfume, felt her hands rubbing his back. "Then what else do you need, my sweet?"

"You don't know what it is to be poor. You'd think differently. It's such a little matter." Her soft white hand covered his penis, massaged it skilfully. "My magnificent master. You shouldn't be bothered with these petty arguments."

One short phrase abruptly repeated in Edward's mind. Richard on a crusade. The only man he trusted. Never. Let London bridge fall. He said sleepily. "I'm not keeping the Neville land."

"Then send Anne Neville away. She's not worth a quarrel." Elizabeth thought with contempt of Richard. She'd never understand why her husband cherished the runt. "The Neville looks barren. A narrow-hipped bitch."

Edward seized his wife. He didn't hear the words. He'd found his wife's vagina lips. He pumped into her until she responded, arching her back, murmuring in her throat.

She'd try another night, Elizabeth thought. Sooner or later, he'd see it her way.

It seemed to Anne she'd been asleep but a few minutes when she was awakened by an urgent shaking. A tiring-woman bent over her. "Lady, oh lady, do wake." The woman shook, terrified. "Your sister, the Duchess Isabel sent me. She's great need of you."

"Isabel?" Anne sat up in bed, pulling on a nightrobe, pushing back her hair. "What's amiss?"

"The duchess be sick." The tiring-woman blinked and added, "Turned red as a lobster."

"Oh, poor Isabel. It's probably the measles. She never had them as a child."

Nan Fitz Hugh squinted at the woman in the darkness. "You're supposed to have come earlier." Nan's voice was thick with sleep.

The woman's head shook back and forth, almost palsied. "No. No. I was told to wait upon the Duchess Isabel. Please, lady, hurry." She grabbed a cloak from a peg. "Here. The duchess be out of her head with fever."

"I'll go with you." Nan sat up in bed.

"No. But thank you. It can't be serious. Clarence is one to panic." Anne pushed her hair under the hood of the cloak. "I'll be back soon."

She followed the tiring-woman through the corridors still lit by an occasional taper, but it was only the woman's torch, an uneven flicker in the night, which showed the way as they hurried from the Upper Ward to the Middle Ward. Anne followed, puzzled. She could dimly see the squat outlines of the Salisbury and Garter Towers, marking the curtain wall and the westmost end of the castle, before the woman stopped in the vastness of the Lower Ward. A night patrol stamped by at a little distance; there was the muted exchange of salutes.

"I thought the Duchess of Clarence was housed in the Upper Ward. Why bring me here?" The girl pulled her cloak closer and shivered. The pounding of the patrol faded.

"Aye. She was." The woman's voice quivered. "The duke arranged for me to take you to the Curfew Tower. Horses and carriage wait there."

"The duke?" Anne tried to see into the darkness.

"O' Clarence, m'lady. His duchess be sick, hot sick. She'd return to London." The woman plucked at Anne's sleeve. "Come. Please. Hurry."

Anne hesitated. Why leave Windsor at all if Isabel was so ill? And in the darkest hours of the night? She crossed her arms and stood still. "I'll wait here. Tell the Duke of Clarence to come to me and explain."

The tiring-woman trembled. By the torchlight her worn face was white and twisted with fear. "Lady," she whispered. "I canna take such a message. I must bring you. That's what he gave me the gold coin for."

Damn Clarence's uncertain temper. A dash to London in the middle of the night was perhaps but a natural, dramatic gesture to him. Anne shrugged and continued to follow as the woman crossed the parade grounds to the Curfew Tower, built long ago in the thirteenth century and often used as a prison.

"Inside," she urged. "His grace said inside."

Anne put her hand on the damp stone surface. "Nay, I'll wait here." She looked up at the sky and wondered at the time. It must have been close to three o'clock. The creeping chill of night closed mistily about the whole Lower Ward. The bells would probably soon ring the hour. Again the woman touched her sleeve.

"Please, my lady. The air's cold. Inside, please."

"No. You may tell the Duke of Clarence I'm here. And where is my sister?"

"Oh, lady, I beg you." The woman grew distraught. "His grace promised me another gold piece if all was done as he ordered. Lady, my child has terrible stomach-pains. With th' gold I'll buy some betony wine an' the white poppy juice. What does it matter if you wait inside? It will be warmer."

"I'll give you a gold noble myself, if I'm here in the

morning. I'm not going to London." Anne heard the watch again and the chilly fear receded. "I am going back," she said bluntly. "Tell George of Clarence to fetch me himself."

She turned and tripped in the darkness. Without a light it was a maze, not of shrubs and flowers, but of blackness and unknown objects and vague shadows. Moving carefully, she started toward the dim silhouette of the Round Tower, one hand outstretched before her, the other holding her cloak.

A torch blazed in the darkness against the west curtain wall and Anne called, "Watch, a light here, if you please."

"No, sister-in-law, you don't need the watch." In quick steps Clarence was by her side, his features distorted by the flickering of the torch. Behind him, hulking shadows, were two of his henchmen.

"You'd frighten me half to death, George." Her uneasiness turned to disgust. George was obviously very drunk. "Where's Isabel?"

"Isabel waits in the coach. Come, Anne." Clarence's words blurred together. He stumbled over the paving-stones.

"Not tonight. Nor should Isabel leave Windsor being sick. She can be attended here."

"Sick. Sick of Woodvilles. Sick of my noble brother." Clarence grasped her arm so hard she flinched. His breath stank of wine. He belched and spewed wine down his chin.

He vomited before drinking more, Anne thought in contempt. There'd be no reasoning with him. She managed to say calmly, "Well, then, George, let's go back to the state apartments and have a drink to warm us on this chill journey. You must tell me which wine is the finest."

Clarence laughed. "Come, little Anne. Come, we're going back to London, and I'll tell you about my noble brother Richard."

She stood still though the pain in her arm was intense. "You're not my guardian any longer, George. Perhaps I'll follow you to London in the morning."

"My would-be heiress, you'll come tonight." The words were a hoarse, hot whisper in her ear.

"No, George, I'll not come." She glanced about, thinking of the hundreds of people sleeping nearby, yet sensing no security. There was a remote quiet at this westmost end of the castle. Anne wondered if Clarence had bribed the guards. She knew the first sharp pricks of real fear. "Where's Isabel?" she asked again.

George nodded to the two burly, blank-faced men wearing his badge. Anne started to run as they half seized her and, twisting free, she plunged into the dark shadows of the night. Crouching against the curtain wall she could hear their low voices and she put her hand over her mouth to quiet her hard breathing. If the watch would but come soon, she could call for help. Her heart beat in her throat and her body trembled with cold and terror, but she dared not move.

Anne gave one startled gasp as the bells of the Curfew Tower chimed the hour and in the same moment the two henchmen seized her. She struggled and pulled and cried aloud. Throughout the castle the bells clamoured. At an order from Clarence one of the servants picked her up and carried her to the Curfew Tower and down the staircase within the walls to the basement, where dampness and age clung heavily to the thirteen-foot-thick walls. Some rusted battle weapons still hung from pegs, for a sally port led from there. All about was the musty smell of disuse and dampness and the quick scurrying of mice as Clarence lit a torch in one of the ancient iron wall brackets. Terrified, Anne stumbled and fell to her knees as the servants put her down. She was going to die, she thought in desperation. He was drunk with wine and rage and he'd kill her.

"Well, Anne Neville, so you kneel." Clarence's voice seemed distant yet she could see the elongated points of his shoes. "I killed your husband. He thought to sit on the throne that should be mine." Clarence's tone grew thoughtful, even puzzled. "But you didn't mourn. Even your uncle, the archbishop, said you didn't mourn." He pulled the girl to her feet. "I did you a favour, did I not, when I stabbed your husband?"

Anne swallowed, fear dry as tinder in her mouth. The scene at Tewkesbury was momentarily more clear than the packed earth and ancient stone.

Clarence laughed. "You are hot for bed with my brother, little doxy. Do you think he loves you? He wants your lands."

She was silent. The estates for the most part were Richard's under the grant from the King whether he married her or not. The rest of the inheritance was the cause of the quarrel.

Suddenly she was jerked closer by her brother-in-law. He breathed down on her, odious and repulsive, but she couldn't draw back. Anne saw he wore a dagger. A small, jewelled toy. It would be enough.

She wondered if any words would penetrate his wine-drenched brain.

"George, if you kill me, you'll pay. Murder. Murder the charge. Death the penalty. Richard's Constable of England."

George laughed. "Death! No, no, dear sister-in-law. Oblivion, a non-existence."

Anne looked at his haggard face in puzzlement.

He enjoyed himself. It was all like a little drama, a fool's play. "And to take with you into oblivion, Anne, know this. Richard fathered two children in the past year. A girl called

Catherine and a boy, newborn, named John."

"He would have told me."

Clarence shrugged. "Perhaps in time. No time left for you, Anne." He jerked her head back, forcing her to look up. "I want to see that knowledge in your eyes, Anne. You can think about it in your lost future." His words blurred together. His grip on the girl slackened. For a moment she thought to run.

George nodded at his servants. "Now."

Pain. Darkness streaked with flashes of light. Then nothing.

VIII

"Hot sheeps' feet, girl?"

A boy of about eight stood over Anne. His nose was running. His upper lip was a mass of scabs. A larger boy at least thirteen sat beside her. He'd pushed aside her clothes and was examining her breasts, rubbing his fingers across the tips. She wondered if the two were part of a disordered dream. Her head ached with throbbing violence. Her body was dull with pain though awareness grew so quickly that in moments she felt her wrists flame with rope-burns. Using all the strength she had, Anne pushed aside the curious young hand. The boys were real enough. "Water," she whispered.

The older one went to a keg and drew a half mug of beer. He sat down beside her and held her head as she sipped it. The room was a cavern of darkness. One taper burned in a wall sconce, dimly showing beer-kegs, possibly wine-casks, and stone crocks. The mattress on which she lay was straw and damp. There was the fetid odour of rat- or mice-droppings.

"Where am I?" Each word was an effort.

"The cookshop." The older boy grinned.

"Your father's?"

"Aye." The younger one still held the sheep's-foot offering. "He'll be by when he's closed up for th' night."

Anne realized she was still in her nightrobe and cloak. It must have been well over twelve hours since Windsor. By now Richard would be looking for her. A sick awareness followed immediately. How could he possibly find her?

The older boy tipped the berr mug and some ran down her chin. He took a deep swallow himself and tried again. "I'm Peter. He's John. Had an auntie, all swell and holy. Christian names she called 'em."

Anne wondered how much the two boys knew. Probably nothing. The father might. She forced words through the haze of pain. "Bread? Soup? Please."

In an instant both boys were up and promising to bring the very best. She heard them drop a crossbolt on the door as they left. They didn't return.

Anne lay on the mattress. So she was a prisoner. She must have been flung across a horse and brought here. That would account for the aching body-pain. Mice rustled in corners. Forcing herself, she fingered the tenderest place on the back of her head. It was still wet. And swollen. She licked the sticky dampness on her fingers. Blood. To bind her wrists had been unnecessary. The room faded into total darkness. Anne wondered if the mice or rats would smell the blood. Clarence's words came in flashes of pain. Richard, two children. God. Even as she endured agony in France. Still, fathering bastards was common enough for unmarried men, and many a married man, too. No one thought much about it. Richard was a prince of the realm, not a saint. Her head ached so. She couldn't bear to move. Oblivion, Clarence had said. A death in life. Would one day at Windsor be all she had to remember? Anne tasted salt tears of silent sobs.

The taper had long since burned out and it was totally dark when the door crashed open. She looked up. Fear gripped her.

He was a stocky man. In a hallway behind him torches cast long shadows from iron sconces. She couldn't see his face.

"So you be Anne o' Warwick." He smelled of mutton an smoke.

"Yes."

"Well, I'm Tom an' that's all ya need to know. This be a cookshop. When you're head's cleared, you'll be doin' kitchen work. We need a hand."

"The Duke of Gloucester ... pay for me."

Tom chuckled. "Girl, the Duke o' Clarence has 'bout made me a rich man to keep you here. An' keep you I will." He stepped closer and sat down beside her. The shadows were still across his face as he pulled her clothes away.

"No. Please." Anne pushed at him.

He laughed and cupped a breast in a rough hand. He played with the soft mound of flesh.

"Scared, Anne o' Warwick?"

Fear closed her throat. She tried to turn. His hand was on her pelvic bones.

"You're a skinny slut." He laughed again, pulled aside his codpiece. "Why, my Betty's got tits twice as big an' a lot more bouncy. No bones to prick either."

Anne closed her eyes. He was huge. A mat of black hair, then the giant piercing thing. "Gloucester. Constable." She forced the words from the depths of her terror.

"Girlie, Gloucester's not goin' find you. How'd you like me to do it to you? I've never had no fancy lady."

Revolted, horrified, Anne lay still. She'd no way to fight or escape. Maybe she would die. Bleed to death.

Tom studied her. Limp. Bony. He yawned. "Yer small for a bitch. I'll give ya to my boy in a bit. He'll be fourteen soon. No sport for him if I tear you to pieces." He scratched and crunched a flea. "So for now this be the way of it. I'm Clarence's man, have been since he set up his own house. A proud young cock. I don't care 'bout feuds an' Warwick against the King, any of the bloody pother. I just go along."

He spoke slowly. The words were rehearsed.

"So it can be this way – you tied up here all the time. It gets mighty damp when its rains. Or you can work in the kitchen just like any cookshop drab an' with no talk. You try talkin' to someone an' you're back down here till you rot."

"I understand."

"An' you'll eat wot my own eats. I got two boys an' a fine wife. You mind her. She don't know you an' she's got a mean hand. Thinks you're some slut the duke wants rid."

She nodded. Even the slightest movement brought waves of pain.

"So up, girlie. An' no tricks."

Anne tried to get up. The pounding in her head enveloped her. Nausea wrenched her empty stomach and she bent forward in a dry coughing spasm. The room whirled. The hall torches became elongated. The dark figure in the doorway shrank slowly in size. A coldness raced down her spine. Cold, so cold. She bent forward and there was hay again. Wondering, she sank into it. Deeper into the darkness ...

The woman who sat beside Anne this time was red of face and hair with the amber eyes of such colouring. The girl watched freckled hands wiping her face and arms and then wearily opened her eyes fully.

"So, dearie, you're mighty sick there."

"I remember." Anne could barely speak. Her tongue was swollen, lips cracked.

The woman dipped a rag in a glass and held it over her mouth. "Open up, an' I'll drip some down. Been doin' that for two days. Think you'd died else."

Anne did as told. Her head felt tied to the mattress.

The woman sat cross-legged beside her and dripped first water then a clear soup. "It's a lot faster now an' you can swallow, girl." She surveyed Anne critically. "Washed and dressed yer, too. An' washed that crack on the head. Three cracks actually. Only one causin' the trouble." She redipped the cloth. "I'm Betty. Tom's Betty. An' he says you're Annie and the duke's tired of you." She shook her head. "But we're to keep you safe case he changes his fancy." She grinned. "He paid us plenty. You must be a lively tumble."

Anne didn't answer. She remembered Clarence on the ship at Calais. He had threatened then. She'd been a fool to let him trap her. Without moving, she said slowly, "Where am I?"

"Why you're in Cheapside, girlie. An' a grand cookshop we got now."

A small hope quickened. London then. Not so far. Clarence had estates all over England and Ireland. She could have been imprisoned in some distant, unknown place. Perhaps Clarence considered this Tom especially reliable.

Betty was regarding her thoughtfully. "Yer got such small, smooth han's. An' fine hair. Were yer a favourite whore?"

Anne thought of Isabel. Clarence's one virtue was his fidelity to her sister. "No. Just a diversion." She realized every word was crucial. "A lady's-maid."

Betty nodded. "And the duchess found you out, I wager." She laughed. "Well, no harm done. You'll heal. Yer must be hungry. 'Tis white bread we got these days. Can you chew?"

"I think so."

"Aye, you're young. You'll mend quick enough."

Anne lay still after Betty left. She'd mend. She tried to summon resolve beyond that. Resolve to escape, to find Richard. Richard, father of two bastards. The will was further than her reach. Too much had happened. She had survived, yet not survived. She was sixteen years old. It was enough. She had seen all of life she cared to see. Lying with her eyes closed in the stillness, she felt an all enveloping fatigue. Striving was useless. Hopes were always shattered. Her heart betrayed. Everyone probably came to such a time except the very, very fortunate and those who never cared. Anne wished fleetingly she could be among the non-caring. Clarence had said her lost future. He was right. Ahead was degredation, rape, a final crushing of her soul. Death was the alternative. She was so weak. Only a lethargic despair stirred sluggishly at the centre of her being.

It was three weeks before Anne could sit up for any length of time. Betty was annoyed. "You best get well faster, girlie. The work be piling up. The pewter needs polishin'." The woman looked tired herself. "You don't be thinkin' you're a fine lady, do you?"

"No, Betty. I just get so dizzy."

"Dizzy or no, it's the kitchen tomorrow."

Anne remembered the dank room below the cookshop. It had been raining for several days. This room, while barely more than a closet, was warm, being over the kitchen. "I'll try. Really."

In the darkness of night she wondered she could care about comforts when she didn't care if she lived or died. Sleep eluded her. With the dawn she'd become in every sense of the term a kitchen drab. Yet so were hundreds, nay thousands, of girls. It wasn't that. Clarence had succeeded. He'd killed hope. Richard would look for her and, not finding her, turn to someone else. Isabel would wonder, but there'd be no answers. Her sister would probably not even suspect George. Nan Fitz Hugh could accuse the tiring-woman who had, no doubt, disappeared. Her mother was probably still in seclusion at Beaulieu Abbey. And the others. The King would be glad his brothers no longer argued. For the first time Anne made a choice. She didn't care to live. She wondered how to die. It would take a weapon. A kitchen knife. Tomorrow she'd take one. Strangely, on that thought, sleep came easily and deeply.

IX

Having searched for Anne in vain, Richard now faced George. He longed to take his brother's fine linen shirt, wrap it around his neck and pull till Clarence turned blue.

"I don't have her, Gloucester." Clarence showed injured innocence. "She must have run away. Did you frighten her?"

"Damn you, George." Richard clouted his older brother and Clarence reeled backwards. "You tricked her. I've heard that much."

"Tricked her to do what?" George held his finger to his jaw. He hadn't any desire to get involved in hand-to-hand combat with Richard. He remembered wrestling as boys. His youngest brother was all muscle. "I'll try and forget you hit me," he pouted.

Richard said quietly. "Suppose I knock every tooth from your head? Will that jar your memory?"

"I've no memory to jar, brother." George looked around at the splendour of The Erber. A new tiled floor had just been installed in the Great Hall. He added six glass windows. "Why would I want to harm, in any way, little Anne? Why, she's Isabel's sister."

And that is why, Richard thought in fury. "Let me see

your household lists, George. The names of everyone you employ. I've Edward's permission so don't whine to him."

In the distance the two men could hear the sounds of Isabel's singing. She had a high, sweet voice, inclined to go flat. "I'd like to see Isabel, too."

"Richard, you're impossible. The lists unfortunately burned in a fire a few nights ago. Scraps are all I could save. And I'd employ no one to hurt or hide Anne. Isabel knows nothing. She's as worried as I am, or you."

Exasperation choked in Richard's throat. He tasted bile and blamed himself. He'd not protected Anne.

"The Woodville trollop might know something." George struggled to be calm. "She doesn't like the Nevilles."

"She wasn't the one who sent for Anne." Richard circled closer to George. He saw himself shadowily reflected in the windows. In the corner of the Hall a green parrot screeched from his perch. He flapped his wings and emptied his bowels. Richard watched the droppings fall to the polished floor. Shit. George was shit.

He grabbed his brother while the bird screamed. "Tell me where she is, George, or I'll beat you bloody."

"You wouldn't dare. You've no proof."

Richard hesitated. True. He didn't have a shred of proof except Nan Fitz Hugh's account of the tiring-woman. It was more a feeling. The knowledge that this brother could abduct Anne and hide her. Not for the first time did he wonder in agony where she was hidden. He pictured her tied in some damp hole, among the rats and mice, dying perhaps of lung-fever. He had to find her.

He took George by the shoulders and shook the taller man. He wanted to put him on the rack, tear him joint from joint until he confessed and led him to Anne. With slow deliberation he slapped George's face back and forth.

Clarence pulled his dagger. "Brother, don't touch me again."

Richard was on him in a second. He grabbed George's wrist, twisted the knife free, bent his arm back, slammed his head against the wall. George howled in pain. "Brother, don't draw on me. Where is she? I'll break your skull."

For George greed overrode pain. "I swear 'fore God, I don't know. Ask the Woodville slut." He tried to think of the gigantic inheritance involved. It was worth a few knocks. Richard detested the Woodvilles. Perhaps he'd take the bait. "You know the Queen would lie. Use my name. Put you on my scent."

"George. My God! Richard?" Isabel, carrying a basket of flower clippings, entered the Hall. She wondered if it might be a friendly tussle. Men enjoyed such sport. Yet George's face was white. The parrot was flapping in agitation. "What's amiss?"

"Do you know where Anne is, Isabel?" Richard still held George's arm and his brother groaned.

"No. I'm worried." Isabel wondered at the scene. George had been very drunk the night Anne disappeared at Windsor. He'd come to bed terribly late. Still, he was often drunk. She'd asked Ankarette if Anne had mentioned she meant to run off and the servant had looked grim and said little. She went and settled the parrot on its perch. She wanted to arrange her flowers, probably the last of the season except for a few more roses.

"George would help find Anne if he could," she said mildly. She believed it.

Richard relaxed his grip. He couldn't beat Clarence to a bloody pulp in front of his wife. "You'll let me know if you hear anything? I'll be back."

Clarence whimpered. "My arm. I'll tell Edward."

Richard laughed. "Do. Next time I'll break it. You can tell him that, too."

Isabel looked from one brother to the other. "It's all some dreadful mistake." Her face brightened. "Anne didn't take anything with her. She'll be back. No woman leaves her clothes behind."

The kitchen was at the north end of the cookshop. Its cone-shaped roof was topped by a louvre for ventilation. The oven was deeply recessed. The spit, turned by the youngest son, had a small stool beside it. A great flesh-axe was attached to one wall near a pestle resting on a big marble mortar. All the implements were gigantic. Tom smiled proudly. "I think to join the Grocers' Company. I'm set so fine."

Tom was a big man. Anne remembered how he'd towered in the doorway of the wine-cellar with the torches behind him. Thick calves, thick arms, thick neck, thick lips. A fine linked collar glistened on massive shoulders. Pleasure with himself suffused his face.

"It's a well regarded company," she said carefully.

"Cock's bones, girlie," Tom was amused. "Fine talk and you'll be noticed. No talk."

"As you say." She looked around. "And what am I to do?"

"Betty'll tell you. I'm thinkin' you know nothin' of cookin' or anythin' else."

"Nothing."

Betty appeared in the dawn's feeble light. "I'll tend her, Tom. She'll learn." In her arms was a pile of fish. "Just brought these. Fresh an' flappin'." She gave Anne a shove. "Here's the cuttin'-board. Heads off. We save them there. In that pile. Still have a few back-door folks, yer know." The girl saw a pile of decaying apple peelings, bones, fish and animal parts, egg-shells, and rat-droppings. "Yes, Betty."

The knife was heavy. It severed the heads neatly. Then Betty fried the rest. A few especially fine fish were first coated with batter. Anne didn't think. After the fish, she cleaned fowl, stirred rotted meat and vegetables together in a heavily spiced stew, washed the morning utensils. Dizziness came and went. Once she almost fell when her foot slipped in blood. The brown serge dress she'd been given to wear became spotted with blood and grease. Her hair, bound under a cap as ordered, escaped in tendrils down her back. She wouldn't let herself faint. When this day of eternity ended, she'd take a knife. The thought drove her through the hours, the weariness beyond knowing. John and Peter were there. They talked but not to her. She could hear laughter and loud voices, sometimes singing, from the outer rooms; but she didn't cross the kitchen doorstep. Her thoughts remained riveted on the knife.

At dark she had it. Hidden beneath her skirt, tied to her leg with a piece of thong. It was easy. There were so many knives. Betty looked at her without suspicion. "Well, Annie, you're not lazy. Tomorrow an' I'll teach yer to stuff sausage. My speciality."

"Yes, Betty."

"Off yer go. Yer look half dead."

Anne walked slowly up the stairs. It was down to minutes now. She washed her hands and face in the common bucket. The family brush lay nearby and for some reason she brushed her skirts trying to clean them.

Alone she sat on the straw pallet and waited. In a few moments everyone would be asleep. How still the house was! The streets outside were quiet, too. A soft rain had begun to fall. Slowly, Anne untied the knife. Her father, they'd told her, had been stabbed in the throat. So had the husband she'd never loved. She ran a finger along the blade of the knife. How would Richard die? Would he ever know of her? A time to live and a time to die. Everyone died. She thought of Isabel's baby and its tiny, cold hand. That was death. Twisted, blank-eyed faces stared at her again from the meadow of Tewkesbury. And that was death. A sudden elation steadied her hand. Never again to know pain or fear or caring. The ultimate escape. The Church taught suicide meant the loss of the soul. Strange she should think of that. She'd not been to confession in over a year. And with a shock she realized she didn't care for churchly doctrine. If they were the beloved children ... No. Neither she nor any were beloved. Not if God was all-powerful. Omnipotent love would not allow such suffering in a world of His own creation. She said softly, "Hail Mary, Mother of God, pray for us sinners now and in the hour of our death." She crossed herself. The ritual was served. She'd done what she could do. Now then. The blade was pointed. Anne put it against the hollow of her throat. Sharp. A little warm blood trickled down. Harder. She could not. The cry of self, the existence awareness, shook her, gripped her, and the knife fell from her hand.

She was. She would be. The silent words were a promise. No easy way waited for her. She couldn't escape. She had a distance yet to walk or run or crawl. Though she might exist only in her own mind, such was enough. Hope. Despair. And still she was. Restless dreams were a fever in her brain all the night. In the morning Anne told Betty of scratching herself while asleep.

X

The days were all the same. The girl's hands grew rough and her skin sallow. Her hair, smelling of smoke, hung limp. Tiny cuts festered on fingers and wrists. Beneath the brown dress her body was stick-like. She tried to eat more, especially the better food, but there was never time. Betty drove her sons hard and, now Anne was considered well, she didn't spare her the stick used on the boys. The welts across the girl's shoulders and buttocks never healed before they were replaced by new ones. She made mistakes. She was never fast enough. One day, not thinking, she let the family bread overrise so that it fell flat and tough. Betty slapped her until Anne's cheeks swelled and her jaw felt broken. It was Tom who stopped the beating.

And it grew colder. Anne thought of the lung-fever in France. Another time would be fatal. She told Tom. "I need more food, and to be warmer. I was sick last year. Unless I'm supposed to get sick ..."

Tom shook his head. "No. No." He was finely dressed these days and went often to the Grocers' Company Hall. He complained about prices, the high-nosed mercers and vintners. His role as a prosperous merchant made him softer. "More food. Another blanket. I'll tell Betty to let up on you." He grew thoughtful. "You're a pretty lass. I wish an' you could serve food."

"I wouldn't need to talk, Tom." She said it thoughtfully. She dared not let him see any eagerness.

"Oh aye. Nor do I serve th' King." He laughed loudly. "But you might see someone you know."

Anne shook her head. "I never lived in London. No one knows me."

"Your father lay dead and naked in St Paul's. Sometimes you look like him. I can see it."

"No one else would." She pushed back her hair. She dared not force the hope.

The next day Tom made up his mind. He dragged her roughly by the arm to her little closet room. She saw sweat on his fat upper lip, the quivering of his chin.

"You stay here, lady. I'll have the boys bring food up."

The simple courtesy jolted her. Something had happened. "But why?"

"By all the saints, lady, the Duke o' Gloucester is tearin' London apart lookin' for you."

"But it's been weeks."

"Aye. An' it was kept right quiet. The Duke o' Clarence swore he had no knowledge of you. So Gloucester sent men with the King's seal to Ireland an' all Clarence's lands. Now he's scrapin' London. Any dolt on the duke's household list ..."

"And you served the Duke of Clarence."

"My thinkin' is he'll burn those lists 'fore Gloucester gets to them."

"Richard of Gloucester is Constable of England. Do you want him finding me here? Think, Tom. Get word to Gloucester. Once safe, I'll not gainsay you."

"I dare not. I tol' you. Clarence. God's nails! The King's brothers." He looked at Anne as if seeing her for the first time. "An' Betty, the boys. Betty, she'd skin me for bein' daft."

Anne didn't answer. There was a very high chance Richard wouldn't find her in the maze of Cheapside.

"Lady, you must eat more. An' your hair. Christ an' the saints. You'll have to go back to the kitchen or the boy's tongues like to wag. I'll tell Betty to ease off. Say the Duke o' Clarence is gettin' hot for you." He was shaking. Circles of perspiration darkened his armpits.

"If you're wise, you'll tell Gloucester."

"Lady, you're dreamin.' Your brother-in-law, he'd kill me sure. All the money."

She nodded. "The Duke of Gloucester may kill you, too."

"I know." With a visible effort Tom gripped his mounting fears. "I'll chance it. Stay in the kitchen, lady."

It was easier after that. Richard was looking. The words were like her heart beating once more. Anne worked only at the lightest tasks. Betty fed her the best fish dipped in the choicest batter. The girl was given a fresh dress, wash water, a sliver of soap and a comb.

Peter, the oldest boy, noticed immediately. "Yer a pretty bitch." He said it critically with adult appraisal.

"I feel better. My head must have healed." Anne pondered if Peter might take a message in secret for her and then dismissed the thought. She knew his price; it was in every glance. Not yet. Possibly she would become desperate enough.

It was on a cold day in early November they heard the commotion in the alley behind the cookshop.

"An' ol' Nick, stew yer in hell, pig!' "

Someone yelled in pain. A thud and splash followed.

Betty cautiously looked out the upper half of the door. A tall ruffian in tattered minstrel garb with a battered sawtry was delivering a second kick to the groin of a fallen man who doubled up.

A scab-faced fellow in russet pulled at the cringing victim

by the heels. "Prison sod. By Cock's bones, we should knife the stones 'neath yer filthy codpiece." He fingered his blade.

The taller one grinned and carefully put aside his small harp to keep it safe. "No nuns to rape. I vow my frien' be right. It'd be a cuttin' service." He brought his foot down with a splash into the gutter filth so it spattered over the fallen man. "Wash yer face. Can't be doin' such good less yer clean."

Anne saw over Betty's shoulder the battered man in the gutter was old and dirty and trying to crawl away from his tormentors.

The man with the knife was on top of him. "Goin' somewhere, Lancastrian? Fond o' rottin' Warwick?" He laughed happily. "Methinks not even Warwick's fancy a man without no stones."

Betty pulled open the lower half of the kitchen door. "In here. Quick."

The two men were startled. The old fellow rolled and landed at their feet, half across the sill. Betty pulled him in and slammed the door.

"Back-door trade," she said. "An' it be shame yer bring on yourself, Thomas Malory."

Outside, after a moment's silence, a sawtry and a pipe struck up the popular tune "Jenkins and Julian".

The old man at their feet grinned with blackened gums. "Food, aye. I've a penny."

Betty took the penny. "A fine knight of the dung-heap," she shrugged and returned to the oven and skillet.

The old man grubbed at the refuse. In one hand he held a decayed fish-head. Apple-peelings dangled from the other.

Anne bent over him, sickened by his stench. "Are you truly Thomas Malory?"

His eyes were bleary. "He's dead."

She understood. "But were you?"

"Aye, a lifetime ago. In Warwickshire. A fine gentleman." He spat. "Don't remember much about him. Oh, such a fine gentleman and scholar."

She saw his feet wrapped in rags. His clothes, a ruin of rips and stains, covered him loosely. A sack over bones. Dirt was ground into his nails, his hair, the crevices of his body. Spittle and decayed food crumbs matted his beard.

Anne went casually to the cask of beer and drew off a cup. "He has another penny, Betty," she said.

The woman nodded. It was the busiest time of day. The spit sizzled, rough voices called from the public rooms.

Anne gave the beer to Malory and, hiding it with her skirt, a piece of white bread. He looked up startled.

She put a finger to her lip and shook her head. His eyes were less dim now. Even as he drank the beer she could see a shadow of the someone he'd been on his face.

He belched, pinched a flea and scratched. Anne moved about the kitchen, waiting. When he was not so hungry, not quite so defeated, she had to try. She saw he watched her even as he continued to pick fleas from his hair and beard.

When Betty was checking the oven, Anne drew close. "Thomas Malory, please listen." He was startled, afraid. "I'm Anne Neville of Warwick. You must tell Richard of Gloucester where I am."

He shrank back against the wall, the remaining refuse spilling into his lap. "Warwick's dead. I saw him."

"Yes. I'm his daughter. You met me once at Middleham."

"Middleham? Was I in prison there? No, it was Colchester Castle and Coleshill. God's nails. I don't remember. Why should I?"

She took a quick glance around. The boys were serving. Betty was too busy to watch. "You told us stories at Middleham. Of King Arthur."

Across the stained face a small flicker of knowledge passed. "When Warwick ruled last winter I lodged in this street. I fought for the Lancastrians, for Warwick. When the King's men find me I'll go to Newgate. So what is Warwick to me?" His head dropped to his shoulders, his eyes closed. "Go away, girl, you're from a dream I once had. I never dream any more."

She shook him. "Malory. Listen. The stories of King Arthur. Remember. I heard you tell those stories to me, to Richard. For the love of God ..."

Malory didn't open his eyes, his mouth sagged. She could barely hear him. "Remember. You were sitting by a boy with dark hair. Cushions. Warmth. No. I died. So I can't remember."

Anne turned from him and began to stir some soup. Betty hadn't to suspect. If anything appeared odd the woman would tell Tom and all would be lost. Malory half lay by the doorway. He snored now. Spittle ran down his beard. One half bared arm was covered with flea-bites. She remembered he'd once represented Warwickshire in Parliament. It was possible to die and still live. Anne knew. She'd spent a moment in that lost land. Too much, life was too much. Yet she had to try. It was a chance.

Malory slept the early afternoon. Betty kicked him aside as she hurried about preparing the last food for the day.

Anne knelt beside him. "The other penny, man." She said loudly. He came awake. Dazed. In that moment his eyes focused on her. He leaned close. "You know, I want to hide behind those stories forever in the eyes of God and men."

He attempted to straighten up, staggered and, holding to the wall, pulled himself to his feet. "I owe you a penny."

Betty turned from her pile of fried meats. "An' you owe me your life."

Malory turned with a swinging motion. "I'll thank you in

my grave." He was out the door.

Anne stood there shattered. He hadn't really remembered. Would he come back?

She looked uneasily at Betty. "Odd," she began. "I didn't understand half of what he said."

Betty wiped her hands on a large apron and, handing the girl a knife, began slicing at the meat. "Cut small pieces, Annie. We're actin' so fine lately. It's like the money would last forever."

She hesitated. "Betty, why did you take in that old man?"

"Oh, we were Lancastrians too, once. Never cared much one way or other. But Tom there he's got to be in fine with his duke. Then the duke up and changes to York. We changed mighty fast." She laughed. "Ol' fellow like him just got confused."

"And he did you a favour or something?"

Betty squinted through smoke-fogged eyes. "I guess you could say so. He had some plate. Good stuff. Stole it, like as not. Gave it to Tom for food. Addled thing to do. Real plate mind you."

"Silver?"

"Aye, a dish an' a chalice, right pretty. We sold it for a grand price. Never know what th' beggar might come up with. He can be quite th' proper fellow when he fancies."

Anne nodded and chopped the meat. It had been a chance. She'd failed. How bloody the meat was! Still, Malory might come back. Tomorrow or the day after. Sometime. Her hands were sticky with blood. Many times before in this kitchen she'd simply wiped them dry. Tonight it was as if the blood couldn't be stemmed.

XI

At Baynard's Castle, the family home in London, Richard cursed himself. He'd handled George like an oaf. No way could he shake secrets from his brother as he had when they were children. He'd been a fool to try. He should have gotten George very drunk and gently pried knowledge out of him, like taking bones from a fish, carefully, one by one, until you had the whole thing. Now George hid from him. He sent word he was sick, feverish, totally unable to talk.

Richard thought with agonized alarm how cold the weather was getting. At Baynard's, surrounded by richness and the waving ostrich-feathers left over from his mother's last visit, he tried to plan. Where else could he search? The houses of London one by one? He might still miss her. And London's citizens were an independent bunch, always quick to assert their rights. Not that he gave a damn now. He'd failed Anne. He'd promised to keep her safe. What if he never found her? How could he go through the years not knowing? His wretchedness turned to self-hate. If she doubted his love, it was his fault. She'd already been through too much. She needed cherishing. He prayed each night for another chance and felt God wouldn't listen when he'd already been given his love and lost her.

He began to organize his men for a house-by-house
search. He knew they grumbled. They'd already been in
every likely place. Richard didn't care. He paid them well.
He was afraid they'd miss Anne even if they saw her. She
might not be able to let them know.

He'd persuaded Edward to let him ask the Queen.
Elizabeth Woodville had seen him in her cushioned and
jewelled solar. Two of her sisters had knelt on either side of
her holding trays of sweetmeats. From the way they
shuffled, Richard knew they'd knelt a long time already.

He bowed. Kissed the Queen's hand. "Anne Neville,
Madame. Do you know where she is?" He'd watched the
Queen's face. He must have been the only man in England
who didn't find her beautiful. She looked like a white cat.

"Gloucester, you've much to learn. Your Neville's a
rabbit-hearted bawd. Off to a rabbit-hole, no doubt. Find
someone worthy of your dukedom." She hoped Anne was
dead. Edward was being stubborn about the land.

She'd picked up a mirror. The interview had been over.
So he'd search. He'd even burrow through the dregs of
Newgate. He couldn't think of Anne as dead, buried
somewhere in the cold earth, rotting. Yet bitterness
inflamed his heart more each day. He wondered it could
keep on beating. On November 22 he heard a commotion in
the courtyard. Without hope he went to investigate.

After evensong, when the streets had grown quiet, Tom
came. Sweat-stains spread in splotches on his new velvet
suit. His eyes were furtive. He sat down heavily and
watched Betty cleaning up. "There's a great bother 'bout
Anne o' Warwick," he said.

Betty slopped water over the floor and began to mop it
down. "Why now? She's been missin' for weeks. Nobles.
Got to be frettin' over some coil. 'Tis not enough we have

peace. Now th' King's brothers war."

Tom regarded her gloomily. "Clarence is no match for Gloucester." His thick lips quivered. "Gloucester be Constable."

"What matter?" Betty slopped the water. "You're Clarence's man and well paid for it. Let them snap at each other. It be nothin' to us."

Tom looked at Anne. "Nothin'."

Betty paused a moment and quizzically regarded her husband. "Been up to some more tricks for his high and mighty?"

"No." Tom stared with disinterest at the supper in front of him.

"London always burstin' with talk." Betty finished with the mop and began stacking pans. "Heard Gloucester had two brats. Not likely he's chasin' all over for some girl. Have any girl he wants seems t' me."

Tom nodded slowly. His hands, clenched on his lap, shook. "Gossip." He picked up a beer-mug and gulped it down. "A pox on them all."

Anne hoped and tried not to. There was a constant sense of Richard's nearness. Yet he couldn't know, she told herself a thousand times. Malory was a confused, drunken man. He wouldn't go to Richard. Even if he tried, he probably wouldn't be taken seriously by Richard's retainers. Yet her cheeks flushed hot and she ate with a new hunger. Calling herself a fool she tried to clean her hair, scrape the dirt from her nails, the stains from her dress. She cursed the hope even as it grew stronger.

It was still dark when Betty woke her, the 23 of November, St Clement's Day. Already bells had begun to ring.

"Annie, get to th' kitchen. Tom wants you." The woman's voice came from the shadowed darkness.

·

"Yes, Betty." Holy Virgin, angels, St Clement, Richard – something was happening. It couldn't even be Prime.

In the kitchen Tom paced about. His jowls bounced against his hunched shoulders. Stubble stood black on grey skin.

"There be men out there. No livery. No faces I've ever seen."

"It's dark yet." Anne let the sentence stand.

Betty looked from the girl to her husband. "Cock's bones! What is this stew?"

"She's Anne o' Warwick." Tom turned so abruptly he bumped the wall, rattling the pans. "Gloucester must know. By all the bleedin' bastards in Hell, how did he find out?"

Betty gasped. "She was never out o' my sight, Tom." She swung on her husband. "So this was the great business. Put yourself 'tween the two dukes."

"Gloucester can't be sure." Tom was suddenly close. "I'll kill her. A small body. No proof."

"They'll tear you to pieces on the rack, man." Anne said each word slowly. "Before they hang you. Richard is in charge of executions."

"He can't know." Tom's voice was a groan.

Betty was white with shock. "Anne o' Warwick." She repeated it half in dread, half in disbelief. "We got t' kill her." The woman grabbed a knife. "She'd die easy, Tom."

"And you will die hard." Anne stood with her back to the cold hearth. "Malory knows me. He told Gloucester as I asked."

"Malory?"

Betty went limp. "You know. Th' old Lancastrian. Plate. Backdoor. Scrap-heap. From Warwickshire. Damn him to Hell."

Tom slumped across the cutting-board. "I never meant

harm. Clarence will ruin me an' I let her go. I swear on my mother's grave, I never meant harm."

Betty was coming round. "We'll tie her up. Hide her. She's guessin' 'bout Malory. Nothing but a sot." Suddenly her face brightened. "He'd not go to Gloucester. He's Newgate bait. She's fakin', Tom."

Tom straighted up. "Aye, the wine-cellar. Lung-fever. She'll be dead, natural as can be, in a few days."

Anne stood very still. She hadn't to show fear. "Let me go and nothing will happen. I'll tell Richard," she used his name with a deliberate soft inflection, "to let you alone."

They both stared at her. Light was coming in the small window now. She raised her face toward it. "Free me. I promise, as Anne of Warwick, you'll not be harmed."

"An' if Clarence finds out?"

"Tell him Gloucester found me. As he soon will. Clarence will not cross his brother further."

Betty still held the knife. "Aye, th' dukes will be well enough. 'Tis us who get th' noose. You should 'ave died." Her eyes were wild.

Anne watched the blade. So sharp. "Betty, don't be a fool." The girl knew she was near to breaking.

The door crashed in. Men were everywhere. Horses. The bells of all London clanged in the room.

"Anne."

She reached to him and he folded her trembling body in his arms. Safe. "Richard. Thank God." She was crying now. She saw as if on some stage cart Tom and Betty being bound with ropes and chains, their faces haggard. Betty screamed over and over. Anne remembered the woman dripping water into her parched mouth. "Richard, they were only tools. The wife didn't know who I was until this morning."

Richard glanced at them and she saw how hard his

expression had become. "Well paid tools, Anne." He nodded to his men. "Take them to Newgate."

Betty screamed for mercy, but Anne didn't listen. "Was it Malory who told you, Richard?"

"Yes. He'd never have gotten past my men, but two fellows I brought from Middleham recognized him." He kissed the girl with tender roughness. "God, Anne, to lose you twice."

He picked her up and carried her to his horse outside. "By every saint, I'll not lose you again."

Richard took Anne to the Collegiate Church of St Martin le Grand, near St Paul's, and the chief sanctuary in London. As such it was crowded with political refugees as well as criminals, debtors and the confused.

She saw none of them. Richard had arranged a chamber should be set aside for her. It was a monk's cell, but comfortable. Aunt Cicely was already there. A bed had replaced the monastic cot, tapestries hung on the walls, a brazier warmed the small room.

Cicely stared at her niece. "Holy Virgin, we need soap and water. And food." She glanced at Richard. "I'll tend her."

"No." Anne clung to Richard. "In a while. Please, just let me be."

"Come back in an hour or two, Mother." Richard kept his arm tightly around her. "Let us alone for a while."

Cicely nodded, for once not talking, and swept out. Two guards stepped into place as the door thudded.

Richard held her, stroking her hair. "It's over, sweeting. You don't need to be afraid. Ever."

All the tears of the last weeks filled her eyes, ran down her cheeks. She held to him and cried as a child, shaking with past fear and anguish. She knew she was filthy. Her hair, he touched so gently, was thick with kitchen grease. Still, she couldn't stop sobbing for a long time.

It was late morning when they finally sat quietly on the edge of the bed. Cicely had returned twice and each time Richard sent her away. Now he took Anne's cut and dirty hands in his. "Sweeting, can you forgive me?"

"There's nothing to forgive."

He shook his head. "All those weeks of suffering. Your father dead. Two bastards. You must have heard of them."

"Could you have changed any of it?" Anne hesitated. "The children, yes, that hurt."

"Anne, it meant nothing except I was lonely. Of course, I'll see to their upbringing. It's the pain you've known." He looked at her scarred hands, the still visible bruise on her cheek. "You're so gentle. You were meant only for gentleness."

"I think, perhaps, pain is our fate." She remembered her night of total despair. "When there's joy we must hold it close. Cherish every moment."

Richard kissed her hands. "Anne, you're the only purity I've ever known. After all that has been, you look at me with trust and love."

"You are Richard. It is enough."

He took from his hand the large emerald seal-ring, set in heavy gold which his brother Edward had given him when he bestowed the dukedom. "Anne, wear this. I want part of me to be always with you." He slipped the ring on the middle finger of her hand where the stone caught the light and glowed with green fire.

"The stone of constancy, Richard."

"Yes, Anne, I've loved you all my life. I will marry you. And care for you. Always."

She traced her fingertips across his face, touched his eyes, the tight line of his mouth. "Richard, know joy in our love. You're my strength, my truth. Let us live every day in love."

He held her to him. "All our lives, Anne. All our lives."

In the afternoon Aunt Cicely and her two maids bathed the girl, combed her hair with perfumes, washed her hands again and again. To what she had already brought Aunt Cicely added a puffy satin quilt, flagons of wine and a great basket of food, a handmirror and cosmetics.

Anne thanked her, feeling better but very tired.

"This is a foul place, niece," she said. "Riff-raff. Scum." She yanked a hearth rug into smoothness. "But safe. Even at Baynard's, where I stay, you couldn't be so protected."

The girl nodded. "Yes, protected."

"Richard was sure he'd find you. After Malory. The old scamp's at Baynard's now. Eating everything in sight. Anyway, my son had this chamber all set for you since late last night. For a man he thought of most everything. My own husband, as St Cecilia is my witness, never guessed how I used to long for a soft pillow or a bar of perfumed soap. He had a coach built for me so I could travel with him. It was lined in blue velvet." Cicely smiled at the memory. "But, God's nails, it was hard as the frozen earth and I was always pregnant." Cicely's heavily ringed hand reached over and touched Richard's emerald. "You're betrothed?"

"Yes, Aunt."

"As is right. Sweet saints, what a bloodline. I cursed George till he turned pale as a fish when he wanted to marry Isabel. I saw the trouble with Warwick brewing. Times change. You carry Beauchamp blood, too. Neville, Beauchamp, Plantagenet. Violent. Valiant. How we race! Race to win. Maybe someday one of us will race to lose. But it will be magnificent."

Anne tried to listen. The words spun in her head.

"You're hungry." Cicely stood up. "Richard wants to join you for supper. He's been waiting." She patted her niece's arm. "You're a strong girl." She was gone with a swishing of skirts.

They ate in contented silence. Anne was too tired for talk. Richard asked only one question. "Clarence abducted you? Nan Fitz Hugh swore it."

The wine was making her very sleepy. "Yes, Clarence."

"Damn him. I'd send him to the Tower to rot forever. The King forbids it. Edward may be galled, but he coddles George. Clarence hints of a great secret and Edward forgives him anything. He orders brotherly love."

"Perhaps his secret threatens Edward. George would dare." She didn't want to think of Clarence. "Will Malory have to go to prison?"

"Edward will insist. I'll see to it the old fellow has warm accommodations, good food. He'll not be put in the common cells."

"I've heard they're naked there. Often insane. Whipped."

"Anyone without money will soon die." Richard spoke flatly.

"What about Betty and Tom? I never knew their proper name."

"Colynbourne. Tom has a brother William who was an officer in my mother's household." Richard shrugged. "They were tools, Anne, as you said. They'll spend the same number of days at Newgate as they kept you prisoner. And pay a fine."

Her eyes were heavy with exhaustion. She forced down a little more food and gave up trying to eat.

Richard lifted her onto the bed. "I'll get some maids to attend you, Anne."

"Wait." She couldn't let him go. She was alone when he

was not with her. "Richard, when can we go back to Middleham?"

"When I have convinced the King's council on a fair division of the inheritance. Soon. I've no patience." His face was bleak. "God and his saints, I want you and to go back to Yorkshire. It's all I've ever wanted."

"A simple dream." Anne had closed her eyes. His hand was warm to hold.

"Yet we can't catch it."

"We will. At Middleham."

Richard kissed her on the lips with hard urgency and then tenderly on the bruised cheek.

"Rest, Anne. In only one day you've given me back hope."

"Sweetheart, we'll give each other hope. In my mind I see us walking through dark forests and stretches of meadow and the dales of home. We're together. I'm content."

"Be content, sweeting. We are together, forever."

During the night the brazier was kept lit and a tiring-woman sat by it. When Anne awoke from the turmoil of her dreams, she could see Richard's emerald in the dim light.

XII

In Newgate Malory heard the screams of a whip-fight. He
dragged himself to the window-slit to watch. Breathing was
hard. A constant pain burned in his stomach. The
December cold stabbed him. Two prisoners, naked,
desperate, fought to kill. He leaned from his cell, the best
one on the upper level. The courtyard swarmed with
prisoners. Their skins were grey with dirt and disease,
splotched with running sores. Some had been brought up
from the lower levels to witness the fight and they blinked in
the sun, slapped their bare hides and clung together for
warmth. Long whips cracked. Two women fought. God.
They screamed. Hair floated about their scarred bodies.
Then one wrapped her whip around a drooping breast of
the other and pulled. In a moment they were on the ground.

"Eyes. Eyes. The eyes, Bessie." The crowd chanted and
cheered.

Bessie slowly gouged out the eyes of her victim. She held
the whip between her teeth, straddled the stomach of her
fallen foe and dug into the soft tissue with her thumbs.

Malory saw the eyes ooze forth, like bloody grapes. The
defeated woman screamed, twisted and tried to bite. Bessie
raised her hands holding dripping tissue. She laughed.

"Well, Sir Thomas, you're comfortable?"

Malory swung around. "Aye. I eat. Sleep. Better than in years." He shaded his own eyes. Richard of Gloucester seemed to blaze. Everything in Newgate was grey except Gloucester. He wore green and gold. To Malory he was as the earth and sun. "And I thank you, your grace. I know how I'd fare without you."

"I've asked my brother to release you. He says in a little while."

"There's not a little while for me, my duke." Malory thought with indifference of the death signs stalking near. Not with a whip or club, but quietly. He went to his one possession, a thick manuscript. "I give this to your care, your grace."

"The legends of Arthur?" Richard remembered hearing them at Middleham.

Malory smiled. "Some night soon I'll dream of that time and go there. Forever." He hoped it would be this night. Life was over. He was ready.

"I'll not forget you saved my lady." Richard picked up the faded and ragged manuscript. "I'll share this with her. And see to your care until you're free."

Malory could feel the beating of his heart, each thump an effort. "Tell Anne, I'm glad I did a favour for her. Gave meaning ..." He sank down on the floor, the racing pain in his chest was too great to bear standing. "Ask Anne ..." His voice blurred " ... pray for me." He slumped.

Richard bent over him. The pulse beat wildly. The old man nodded as though in contentment. "Take the manuscript. Go." The grey head slumped forward.

Richard crossed himself and held the legends close.

Malory's voice rattled in his throat. In one suspended moment he remembered himself as a boy in Warwick. The legends had haunted him even then. His face became peaceful. He looked beyond Richard and Newgate and time. "I'm free," he said clearly. And died.

In sanctuary Anne knelt to receive Friar Michael Lynn's blessing. He'd been sent to her by the Duchess of York. He was a Grey Monk, a Cistercian; their giant abbeys filled the north. Still, she'd been wary. Yet, he'd not talked to her of sin but of redemption. Of a God who couldn't be diminished to a place where humans understood. "You must believe in faith," he'd said, not sternly but with the burr of East Anglia and a gentle compassion.

She'd turned away. "Do you know of Angers?" The hidden agony had tumbled out. "They've a piece of the true cross there. I vowed on it. I haven't prayed since. Prayer does nothing."

"You must have faith, daughter." The concern had shown in his dark eyes, the flush of his cheeks. "As a boy I lived near the shrine at Walsingham. I saw so many like you. Sad. Lost. Yet they were found."

"Faith is grace. Grace is a gift I've not received." Anne had watched him, waiting for demands of penance.

"You love." Michael Lynn leaned forward. "A small light in the infinite light." His wooden rosary had swung in his hand. "I'll pray for you, my child."

Almost as a reflex she'd said timidly, "Bless me, father."

She was still warmed by his blessing when Richard came. She accepted Malory's death in sadness and listened with serenity to reports of Clarence's continued demands.

"Everything must be settled with Clarence or he'll make trouble. Even for our heirs." She leaned close to Richard. How warm the small room was. Distantly they could hear the scufflings and murmurs of St Martin le Grand. She alone in that giant sanctuary had privacy. She kissed Richard. "I'll be patient. Isabel sent my clothes from The

Erber." Among the dresses had been her mother's coral rosary. A good omen for this day.

"Sweeting, I've brought you a present." Richard motioned to one of the squires who guarded the door. He carried what appeared to be a monstrous paddle wrapped in a blanket.

"What Yuletide trick?"

"No trick, sweeting. See cleaned, rewired and beribbonned ..." He pulled away the blanket.

"My lute!" She hugged it. "You sent to Warwick for it." The green ribbons twined through her fingers. "Ah, but I'm rusty. I've not played."

"And now you must." Richard's lips brushed her hair. "We've no other singers."

Slowly Anne adjusted the pegs of the wire strings, humming and listening. Her pale gold hair fell across Richard's doublet and he curled a piece through his fingers. She let the day's contentment fill her. She was safe. Perhaps God cared. She'd try and pray for Malory and keep his legends secure. The song was from the days at Middleham.

"Weep no more, weep no more
Flowers bloom on a northern moor."

Richard held her tightly. He looked so young and strong.

"And I will dry my eyes, dry my eyes,
For love was born in paradise."

She wondered why she ever worried. The legal squabble with Clarence, the malevolent Woodville court. Such didn't matter. They'd soon cross those northern moors.

The third week in February, about midday, the message

came in Richard's clear handwriting. "Dress warmly and well, with jewels, sweeting. We can marry. R."

The lassitude of the last weeks fled in one joyous flush. Her hands trembled as she turned over the content of the coffer for her favourite gown. The dress from Windsor was designed for summer. Nevertheless she'd wear it. And the collar. Anne sent a quick mental thanks to Aunt Cicely for the mirror and cosmetics. She had to look her best, oh sweet saints, she'd never before wanted to look so fine.

She was still combing her hair so it fell in waves down her back, when there was a lively commotion in the corridor. The knock was a command. She opened the door, expecting Richard, and drew a startled breath. King Edward stood there in his favourite gold and red and smiled at her.

"Your grace." She knelt.

He lifted her quickly. "Don't kneel to anyone except God, Anne Neville."

She stared at him.

"It's proper. I escort you to your wedding, Anne." He made no move. "Also, you should know that Richard has fought a bitter battle to win you. He relinquished his position as Great Chamberlain of England for the simple office of Warden of the Royal Forests beyond Trent. He let Clarence have Warwick castle in order to keep peace. He understands it's wise not to anger George. I think he'd have let him have all but Middleham, if needs be."

Anne stood stunned. "Your grace, I don't know why Richard cares for me so."

The hard remote expression faded from Edward's face. "Because you look in a delicate way like your father, whom we both loved. Even to Barnet. Because you've survived a year filled with hate and betrayal and can still give love. Because you have cared for each other since childhood."

She nodded. "Yes, Richard is my verity."

"A fortunate man. I've never been that to anyone. Nor ever shall. Long ago, there was a chance." Edward stopped. "Horses await, Lady Anne. I'm to take you to Westminster Abbey."

"Sire." She swallowed and plunged on. "Richard is totally loyal to you."

He smiled and the bitterness was back in his face. "I know, Anne, I am his tarnished god."

They rode through the streets of London. The King's squires had brought fur wraps for her. She heard the people cheering the King. Several times there was a murmur: "A Warwick." Anne didn't know any face or indeed the streets themselves.

At the Abbey the King helped her from the horse and led her into the vast nave. The cathedral was lit by the pale glimmer of the February day. The flag of St George with its cross, red as the holy martyr's blood against the white field, stirred in the chill draughts blowing about the nave. Edward led her directly to the chapel of the Confessor and said she should wait a moment for the service to begin. Anne nodded, accepting. It was very quiet. The Confessor's shrine of Purbeck marble gleamed with its inlay of gold and glass mosaic. Tombs all around. Edward III, common ancestor to all of them. And Richard II with the long, narrow face and beard whose effigy stared upward with contemplative, half-closed eyes as though dreaming forever of the crown he'd lost. About the tomb of Eleanor of Castile candles burned as they had for almost two hundred years. From here, too, she could see the silver-plated effigy of Henry V, covering in splendour the sarcophagus of the victor of Agincourt. So they all rested, or did not rest. Many had waited in the Confessor's shrine, for weddings, for coronations. She wondered if any part of their being lingered in such a place where their lives had changed.

Then Richard was there and putting her hand in the formal manner on his as he led her to the altar in front of the chapel. Anne had one quick glance at a small group gathered in the choir, saw Uncle George as Archbishop of York standing uneasily at the altar and then knelt with Richard by her side. Unconcernedly she realized they had never received a dispensation. She didn't care. They'd won through to this day.

They said their vows. The archbishop began the wedding Mass. He moved as an old man, nor did he look beyond the limits of the sanctuary. His twitching eyes stared down at the Holy Eucharist. The Latin phrases were familiar: "*Hoc Est Enim Corpus Meum ... Hic Est Enim Calix Sanguinis Mei ...*"

Anne lifted her eyes no higher than the lace hem of his embroidered alb. Forcing her hand to be steady, she took Holy Communion and looked with shy hope at the suffering Saviour on the cross who in some miraculous way was a part of this bread and this wine. She wanted to pray. Tears filled her eyes, emotion broke through, her heart pleaded, "Oh, abide with us. Bless us. Have mercy." There was a ringing of bells, the familiar words of the *Paternoster*.

Uncle George bestowed the nuptial blessing. Richard assisted his bride to her feet and lifted her face for a kiss. One flesh, she thought, her body yielding to his embrace. The joy of her youth. The joy of her life. She smiled at him. "All's well, my love."

"Sweeting." Richard kept his arm about her even as he drew back a little to better see her face. "Anne. Always you and you alone."

XIII

The ceremony over Uncle George nodded, mumbled paternally and with a flourish of his robes bestowed a kiss on his niece's forehead and bowed toward the King.

Edward didn't return the salutation. Already, with his long strides, he had come from the choir to the altar, and, bending, kissed Anne full on the mouth. "Welcome, sister, Duchess of Gloucester, to the House of York. May the stars watch over you."

"Thank you, Sire."

He turned to Richard. He wished he could command his brother and Anne to never change, never grow old, never become cynical. Perhaps in Yorkshire they'd find a place for their hearts and be at peace with life. He said only, "You are blessed in this woman, Dick."

"I know." Richard looked from the brother he'd faithfully served to his wife. "The world has come right again. We thank you, Edward."

"And may God bless your marriage-bed and make it fruitful." Elizabeth Woodville, appearing cold and somewhat hastily dressed, joined her husband and stared at Anne's narrow hips. Thank the angels the chit was leaving London. The Queen admitted Anne's beauty to herself.

"Thank you, Madame." The new Duchess of Gloucester didn't curtsey.

Richard kissed the slim white hand of the Queen. "And may your own royal children grow in health."

Elizabeth arched a thin eyebrow. "They will, Gloucester. They will."

Richard bowed again. "If you'll excuse me, Madame, Edward, I'd like to greet the other guests." Slipping his bride's hand through his arm, he led her down the length of the choir. She could hear Elizabeth Woodville's whisper: "Just like her father. Damn her."

George and Isabel stood by obviously unsure of their welcome. With sudden joyous impetuosity, Anne hugged Isabel. Her sister looked frailer than she remembered. Wan.

George of Clarence slapped an older brother's hand on Richard's shoulder. The inheritance problems had been settled to George's satisfaction. The past was forgotten. "Well, may St Raphael watch over you both."

Isabel turned to Richard. "Come back with us to The Erber so we may taost your nuptials. I've no special banquet planned. It was all so sudden." She paused and glanced at her husband.

"I don't think so, Isabel. Edward suggested we come to Westminster for some festivities. But Anne and I would prefer to be alone." He looked at Clarence. "We have been kept much apart. I'll not forget by whom."

"Isabel." Anne hated to let go her sister's cold hand. "You must come to Middleham. Soon."

"I might, Anne." How tired Isabel sounded! Perhaps it was the wintery chill.

The door of the nave had been opened and an icy February wind blew into the very centre of the Abbey. Richard put a cloak about Anne's shoulders. She heard him saying something to the small group about the honour and pleasure of having them come on such short notice.

Of a sudden the giant bells of the Abbey began to ring in a clamorous cadence, heightened and carried by the wind. Richard squeezed her hand and smiled down at her. "They ring for us today, Anne."

She listened proudly. "The bells of Westminster. May they bring us luck, Richard. I wonder who they'll ring for next." She laughed. The coldness had gone. "And what does it matter to us? There're some of your meinie. Can we leave now?"

Richard helped her on a finely caparisoned mare with tiny bells jingling from the saddle. Anne looked back at the Abbey and the group of people now standing beneath the vaulted portals of the west entrance. They seemed small, even to the King who was watching Richard with open affection and Isabel who waved. Anne waved back at them all. "Farewell."

Edward's voice cut through the others. "Godspeed."

Richard took her to Baynard's Castle. Careful not to rush her, he pointed out the original foundations which dated from one of the soldiers of William the Conqueror. "It's stood here banking the Thames at the foot of St Andrew's Hill all those centuries." He watched Anne's face. He wanted her to know he'd be patient. "It burned once, but Humphrey of Gloucester rebuilt it. It was here Edward accepted the crown."

Anne nodded. She'd dreamed so long. A faint disquiet made her pensive. How could their union be perfect as a dream? "And that's the spire of St Paul's?" she asked without interest.

"Yes. Come, I'll show you my chambers. They're on the Thames side."

Anne surveyed the low-roofed solar with pleasure. A fire was already burning in a wide stone fireplace where brass-decorated andirons, tongs and bellows shone with a dull yellow glow. A servant hurried about lighting candles, each one brightening the room, for the early darkness of evening already closed about the city. Anne touched the large, heavy writing table, covered with parchments, quill pens and some scattered blotting-sand. There was a window-seat on the river's side. A woven wool rug covered the centre of the tiled floor in hues of amber and moss-green. The bed and all the furniture was plain, solid oak, unadorned. A stone escutcheon with Richard's emblem of the White Boar hung above the fireplace. Wall tapestries featured outdoor scenes, one showed a castle which stood alone in a world of green. On a large chest in the corner she saw her own belongings, brought from St Martin's, piled next to the wall pegs on which hung Richard's armour and sword. There were the fresh, male scents of bergamot and sandalwood and the warm crackling fire.

Richard looked at her thoughtfully. "Would you prefer we use my mother's solar? She's at Fotheringhay now. In her suite it's all gilt and pearls and white roses with ostrich-feathers everywhere."

"My husband, this is your room." Anne moved quickly to the fireplace and held chilled hands over the heat. "And so I'm at home."

Later when they had eaten supper and the servants had retired, they sat on pillows of deep brown velvet before the fire. A tiring-woman had helped Anne wash and change in the adjoining garderobe; now the girl's long hair fell unbound over a blue chamber-robe. From a gold wrought hanap, emblazoned with the Plantagenet crest, they shared sweet, fragrant wine and laughed and whispered love words. Richard was so close his hair brushed her face.

"Anne, so beautiful." His eyes were dark blue, his face younger than twenty. Softly he kissed her shoulder. "You're like a song, springtime, almond-blossoms."

With one finger she traced the line of his jaw, the curve of his mouth and arch of his cheekbones. "I'm happy, Richard."

He held her hand against his face. "I thought this could never be."

"I know."

He picked up a strand of her hair and brought it to his lips. "Anne, my sweet desire."

She leaned her head against his shoulder.

He kissed her forehead, her lips. "Anne ... wife."

She smiled at him. "Yours, Richard."

Quickly he undid the lacing of the dressing-gown and kissed her breasts. She was aware she trembled though not in fear. His body was so close and warm. She coud feel the hair on his chest as he moved against her, the hard muscles of his stomach and thighs. Everything glowed by the fire. Everything was warm. He caressed the length of her body with his hand, his lips. Her mouth opened in joy under his kisses. A demanding need burned hot as the fire, a need she had not known existed. Her hands reached the centre of his back, pulling him toward her.

"I love you, Anne," he murmured. "Love, all my life."

Passionately she held to him, finding undreamed ecstasy. In moments of long, rapturous joy they became one flesh, each fulfilling the other.

When spring arrived suddenly in March, they left London and rode North. Past Barnet and St Albans, to Leicester and Nottingham. Still North to Pontefract and finally Fountains Abbey, the entrance to the Dales. All the way a warm March wind followed them, as though the sweet April of Chaucer's promise had come early so they might return home.

They never looked back. All life stretched ahead. A number of Richard's retainers as well as Friar Michael Lynn travelled with them. They sang as they rode. When they saw some early periwinkles in pink bloom, Richard placed one in his hat and one in the curve of Anne's bodice. From Fountains Abbey's immensity they travelled the short way to Jervaulx where they were served by their Hospitarim "as though they were Christ Himself" for such was the abbey's motto. Sometimes at Middleham Anne remembered hearing the bells of Jervaulx. She knew her parents had often donated to its infirmary. She felt a lightness in her being, home, in a few more miles, home. The monks encouraged them to stay the night. She could not. There was still time to get to Middleham. She smiled at Richard in silent pleading, and he knew, and they went on.

"Journey's end." Anne said it softly. She'd told herself the castle couldn't be as she remembered. Yet it was.

The western sun sent slanting rays of pale gold so the towers cast lengthening shadows, while Middleham stood in perfection welcoming them. They rode around to the northeast entrance. Stone sentinels, silent, weathered friends from childhood, stared down at them. Granite walls soared in crenelated proudness. A fortress since before the Conquest, Anne's ancestor Robert Neville of Raby had built the present castle in the thirteenth century. There had been great marriages, broods of handsome children. Each generation had added and changed the castle. The ashlar-faced walls of the Norman Keep were ten to twelve feet thick and over one hundred feet in length. The Great Hall with its gabled roof and old-fashioned central fireplace could feed and house two hundred and fifty individuals.

Pride in Middleham was her birthright. Now fresh bread
would be baked again, the forges clang, candles burn in the
chapel. Anne drew a deep breath. "I never knew I was so
homesick."

The windlass creaked, the drawbridge lowered in stately
welcome. She felt a racing excitement as the portcullis of
the inner arch rose. The constable of the castle and several
stewards bowed. In an instant the courtyard filled with men
and horses. Pages brought mounting-blocks, grooms
attended to bridles and weary horses. Anne realized
Richard must have arranged all this in advance of their
coming. She glanced up at the outdoor stairway which ran
along the east side of the Keep. There her mother had
always stood to greet her father. For a moment she blinked
back tears. She shouldn't weep. All had been happiness
here.

Slowly she dismounted from her horse and walked the
final steps. With her right hand she touched the great-
walled Keep. She inhaled the smell of leather, horses, sweat
and dust. So many familiar faces. Soon her mother would
join them. Richard was by her side, amidst the turmoil of
arriving, watching her.

Anne took his hand and joined it with hers upon the
ancient wall. "Here, Richard, we will find such joy. I'll
bear your children. And we'll know completeness."

Richard nodded, understanding gentle on his face.

She kissed his hand. "May we never leave."

Richard drew her close. "Sweeting, we may travel, York,
London, but you're right. We'll never leave here." He
looked about and a new bright expression, like a candle lit
within, suffused his face. "Anne, I hope, no believe, we are
here today and through time."

"Yes." She held to her husband. "In some way we have
found our forever place."